ONE DARK NIGHT

Other Collections by Kathleen Blease

Love in Verse:
Classic Poems of the Heart

A Mother's Love:
Classic Poems Celebrating the Maternal Heart

A Friend Is Forever:
Precious Poems That Celebrate the Beauty of Friendship

ONE DARK NIGHT

13 MASTERPIECES
OF THE MACABRE

COLLECTED BY
KATHLEEN BLEASE

BALLANTINE BOOKS • NEW YORK

For an old soul with a grand spirit,
Roger

$\mathcal{M}$y sincere gratitude goes once again to my long-time friend and colleague Elizabeth Zack at The Ballantine Publishing Group. I was thrilled when Elizabeth offered this project to me, and it's been great fun putting it together.

Of course, this manuscript would not exist without the encouragement and aid of my husband, Roger Blease, a collector of rare books and great literature and an outstanding writer and editor in his own right. As I spent countless hours reading scores of stories, Roger was my assistant in culling those that would fit my book best. Every editor should be so lucky to have such capable and intelligent help at her side.

And, finally, I cannot pass this opportunity to thank the classic writers who continue to fascinate me. It is easy to see how an entire lifetime could be dedicated to studying the masterpieces that fill countless volumes. With the masters' works in our hands, this world remains a wondrous place.

Table of Contents

Introduction   xi

"The Face"
by Lennox Robinson   1

"The Dead Smile"
by F. Marion Crawford   11

"A Ghost Story"
by Mark Twain   41

"The Judge's House"
by Bram Stoker   51

"The Tell-Tale Heart"
by Edgar Allan Poe   79

"The Cold Embrace"
by Mary Elizabeth Braddon   89

"The Cedar Closet"
by Lafcadio Hearn   103

"The Adventure of the German Student"
by Washington Irving   119

"The Lost Room"
by Fitz-James O'Brien   129

"An Occurrence at Owl Creek Bridge (Excerpt)"
by Ambrose Bierce   153

"The Dead Girl"
by Guy de Maupassant   167

"The Story of the Inexperienced Ghost"
by H. G. Wells   177

"The Return"
by R. Murray Gilchrist   197

About the Compiler   207

Introduction

One of my favorite games with my two little boys is simply called "our imaginations." My little one prefers to be a triceratops, and a lovable one at that. But my older son treads about the house on his toes in a convincing cadence of the T-rex, with a roar and gnashing of teeth as daunting as a four-year-old can muster. Their play eventually grows into their own childlike brand of story with character, setting, and plot. The T-rex, true to form, usually wins whatever sort of conflict the boys devise. Watching my boys work through their antics makes me wonder where the great writers, particularly the masters of the macabre, began their quest for the ultimate imaginary set of circumstances. Just how did Lennox Robinson come up with the idea of a woman's image peering out from below the ripple of a lake? Not her reflection, but her image, as though she were looking out a window, suspended there for twenty years before she came to life to love and haunt Robinson's hero.

The wonder of the macabre, to me, is how the natural meets the unnatural and just where and how the line is drawn. Sometimes, the mind turns the natural unnatural, then the unnatural natural. And it all seems, well, perfectly natural when the literary masters take it to pen. It's the ultimate stretch of our imaginations.

Just *how* can this happen? It is the human spirit that makes this possible and, of course, our willingness to investigate possibilities. Even if something seems *improbable*, most of us are willing to say that nothing is *impossible*. Indeed, the element of the spirit is addressed in all of

literature, but in the macabre it undergoes a unique meta-
morphosis. It is taken to task, broken out of a mold, and
put through horrific circumstances. Sometimes it is crushed
in the end. Other times it is reshaped and redefined and
seems barely containable. Either way, the macabre ad-
dresses the human spirit as a piece of matter, the same
as flesh, made of atoms. In *One Dark Night*, you'll meet
spirits that stick to the woodwork, hide inside walls, get
trapped in rooms, and sometimes trapped in a mind (of
all places). But the atoms in these soulful entities, unlike
in other fiction, can be easily arranged and rearranged
with just a twitch in the plot. Timeless. Remarkably in-
triguing. And the possibilities are endless.

Researching *One Dark Night* could have been called
a pleasurable scourge. What a luxury to spend dozens of
evenings with the grand, heady inventions of the macabre
masters. What a nightmare to choose only thirteen! I do
believe I spent most of my time happily devouring a
plethora of stories only to put most of them on a pile
called Another Collection Someday.

Finally, the stories that have made it between these
covers represent a certain quality of horror fiction. I was
in search of tales that go beyond the typical ghost story
and do more than make your hair stand on end—much
more—and I believe I found them. Some are familiar and
favorites, others are virtually unknown. These thirteen
brilliant authors take only a few pages to deftly pit man's
human frailties against his divine strengths, qualities that
usually arrive in tandem and scare the hell out of us!
Quite a journey within the innocent form of the short
story.

More simply, perhaps these writers attempted to remind us that since anything is possible, then any *thing* is possible. Any task. Any belief. Any circumstance. Any evil. Any good. It is possible.

Kathleen Blease
Easton, Pennsylvania

The Face

Lennox Robinson
(1886–1958)

Long associated with the Abbey Theatre in Dublin, Lennox
Robinson was best known as one of Ireland's finest playwrights.
He also wrote novels, biographies, dramatic criticism, and tales
of the supernatural. "The Face" is an experiment that explores what
the mind can conjure, develop, make real. The reader and young
Jerry Sullivan alike are pulled into this place where the mysterious
becomes tangible. This is my favorite story in *One Dark Night*.

*N*ever in the daytime or in bright sunlight could you see it, but sometimes just before sunset when some sinking ray of the sun was reflected from the rock to the lake's dark surface, and always in moonlight and on clear starry nights then, lying flat on the top of the cliff and peering over you could see the face quite clearly.

It lay in the deep pool at the foot of the cliff, a few yards from the shore and apparently a foot or two deep in the water. First it appeared as a piece of white rock with a film of lakeweed floating across it, then gradually your vision cleared and you saw the pale features distinctly, the closed eyes and the long dark lashes, the curved eyebrows, the gentle mouth and the fair hair which half hid the white neck and which sometimes drifted like a veil across the face; below the neck the pool lay in deeper shadow, and no one had ever been able to tell the shape of the beautiful creature that lay there.

It was a precipitous climb down the face of the cliff and no one but Jerry Sullivan had ventured it, but as he touched with his fingers the water of the pool the face shivered away, and stretching his arm deep into the water it met nothing except a tendril of lakeweed. Only once had he climbed down because he was afraid that if he probed too deeply the face would disappear forever— for it was days after he touched the water before he saw it again; for the future he was content to gaze at it from above.

He had known it all his life. He could not have been more than six years old when his father had led him to the cliff's edge and shown him the sleeping face in the water. He had never been afraid of it as were some of the other boys; on the contrary when he was sent to drive the sheep from one hill to another he would contrive to pass the lake either coming or going, he would loiter there until the sun sank and risk a scolding when he got home; but hardly a week passed without his seeing the face.

Up among those lonely mountains he saw few women. There was only his mother, old now and grey, and a mile or two to the west the MacCarthys' cottage with the two girls Peg and Ellen, coarsely featured both with thick black hair, and the few other women he saw from time to time were either coarsely dark or foxy red. Was it any wonder that he turned from them to the fair face floating in the water? any wonder that as he grew older he judged every woman's face by that hard standard and found them all wanting?

His father died when he was eighteen years old and Jerry lived on with his mother, tilling the little bit of land, cutting turf on the side of the mountain, driving the sheep. It was a lonely, silent life—for he was an only child—and his mother often urged him to take a wife, but he made the excuse that while she was there he wanted no other woman in the house, and though she remonstrated with him she was well content to remain sole mistress of the cottage to the day of her death. He never told her of those hours he spent by the lake; hidden in a fold of the hills, no one saw him go there, the neighbors shunned the

place as haunted, and as the years crept by the face grew
to be more and more particularly his own.

Fifteen years after his father's death his mother died,
and when the funeral was over he climbed the mountain
and stared for a long time into the water. It was a stormy
winter evening and as the sun went down a pale young
moon appeared. Never had the face been so clear, never
had it looked more lovely. He had felt very lonely when
the earth was thrown on his mother's coffin, now he felt
quietly content. He had nothing left in the world to love
except this face. It had no rival now, he could pour out
all the love of his heart in adoration of it.

And so for three years it went on like this: more and
more he shunned the neighbors, more and more time
he spent by the lake. He began to neglect the farm, for
what pleasure was there in working only for himself?
and to the overtures of the matchmakers he was either
morosely silent or roughly violent. He spent now whole
nights on the cliff; sometimes he thought he saw a stirring
of the eyelids and the fancy grew in him that after sufficient concentration of devotion on his part the eyes would
open; already the cheeks seemed less pale, the mouth
had parted slightly, he thought he saw a gleam of white
teeth.

He grew worn with watching. The woman in the water seemed to draw her vitality from him, and as her
cheeks grew fuller his own grew thin, and as her face
flushed his paled until one evening gazing down at those
closed eyes he saw the lids stir and stir again and at last
very slowly they opened. The eyes behind them were
dazzlingly blue and they met his grey ones with a long
comprehending look. Everything he had ever hoped to

see in a woman's eyes was there, and half in terror, half in joy, he gave a cry and drew back from the cliff; when he looked again a second later the face had vanished.

He thought he would see it the next night, but he looked in vain. He was frantic. There had been weeks before when on account of the weather or some trick of light he had been unable to see the face, but always through those dark days he had been conscious that it was waiting for him in the water, ready to reappear at any moment; now he was only conscious of a great blank, an emptiness, a desolation. He ran round the lake like a distracted man, he looked into other pools—in vain. With the opening of her eyes she had fled and the little lake was as deserted as a last year's nest.

It was three days later at the fair of Coolmore that he found her. She was standing with her back to the wall outside the post-office, and a little curious crowd was round her questioning her and touching her clothes. There was a strangeness, a foreignness about her, and when the village policeman came and began to question her the crowd gathered closer, but her replies were incoherent. She did not know her name or where she had come from or where she was going. She stood there lonely and aloof and her blue eyes kept searching every face piteously, like a blind man feeling with his stick for the pavement's edge. Then she lifted her eyes and beyond the fringe of the crowd they met Jerry's eyes. He again saw that look, he strode to her pushing the crowd away roughly to right and left, he put his arm into hers and led her to his house.

The priest married them and they lived in perfect contentment and happiness. She had been pale and fragile when he brought her home, but she grew every day stronger and more beautiful. She knew nothing of house-work or farmwork and learned but little, preferring to sit in the shadow of a rock in the field while Jerry worked and in the winter to crouch in the corner near the fire or sit in the window in the moonlight. He was quite content to have her so and gladly did the work of two; he liked the mystery of her, he liked to feel her different from the neighbors. She never could tell him where she came from and he soon ceased to question her; he told her of the face in the water, but it seemed to awaken no memory in her mind, and yet sometimes, looking at her—especially when she sat in the moonlight—the texture of her body would seem to become fluidic, her face would appear as if floating, and behind it he would seem to see that other face with its closed eyes. That face had disappeared from the lake and he never went to the cliff now.

In the second November after their marriage when the moon was full a child was born to them, a child as fragile as a moon-ray, that lay in the cradle hardly stirring, never crying.

The fair of Coolmore was held ten days later and Jerry had to bring some cattle to it to sell. Coolmore lay fifteen miles away across the mountain, and he got up very early in the morning, lit the fire, left food and drink for his wife, and started. Peg MacCarthy had promised to look in at her once or twice during the day and he knew she would want for nothing.

He sold his cattle, but there was a delay about pay-ment and it was after four o'clock when he left Coolmore village. He walked quickly, the money was heavy in his pocket, his mind was strangely anxious about his wife and he made the best pace he could. The evening grew colder and colder, yellowish-grey clouds came up from the northeast, the rushes in the lonely bogs bent to the wind, and as he reached the top of the pass it began to snow. It was early in the year for snow, but this was a heavy shower and the big flakes half blinded him as he pushed doggedly on. But his boots grew clogged, he had to walk more and more slowly, and when he was three miles from home he determined to take a shortcut across the hills which would shorten his road by half a mile. It was wild walking but he knew every foot of the path, it led him along the top of the cliff above the lake, and he stopped for a minute there to get his breath. The snow had ceased to fall, the sky was clearing, a few stars shone out and the lake lay black at his feet. Something—old habit perhaps—made him fall on his knees and peer over, and there in the pool below he saw the face. It was there just as it had always been with closed eyes and floating hair. He rose to his feet vaguely troubled. He had never seen it since his marriage.

Half a mile from his house he met Peg MacCarthy walking quickly toward him. "Thank God it's yourself, Jerry," she said. "The wife, God help me, is gone. I saw her just before milking time and she was sitting by the fire. I said you'd have a bad walk home and she said she wished she could go and meet you. Then afterwards, and I sitting at my tea, a step passed on the road and now when I went to your house she's gone."

Hardly stopping to answer her he ran home. It was true, she was not there. The child lay quietly sleeping in its cradle. Then he thought of the face in the lake and he ran up the road and along the path and over the breast of the hill to the cliff's edge. The face was there still, and again as he had done years before he climbed down to the rock. He still saw the face, he touched the water, the face did not vanish, he plunged in his arms and drew his wife's body to the shore.

In the water the face had appeared living, out of it with the wet hair clinging about it, it was cold and dead. Had she come to meet him and fallen in? He could see no hurt on her. Or had she fled from him back to the element to which she belonged? The wet form in his arms seemed less his than the woman in the water. Every impulse of his nature urged him to lay her back. He did so and she sank in the deep pool till only her face was seen.

He climbed the cliff and walked home. He felt strangely bewildered. He hardly grieved. Had he lost her or had he ever had her? Was this only the evening of his mother's funeral and had he, kneeling on that cliff, fallen into a dream and dreamed of the face's awakening, of the marriage, of the child? No, this last was real at any rate, and he took it from the cradle and held it in his arms and stood by the window looking out at the dying moon. And yet—was it only fancy—or, as the sickly moon sank did the child really grow lighter and lighter in his arms, and would he find when morning broke that he was only clasping a tangle of wet lakeweed wrapped in an old quilt?

The Dead Smile

F. Marion Crawford
(1854–1909)

Francis Marion Crawford was born in Bagni di Lucca, Italy, the
son of the popular American sculptor Thomas Crawford. The
young Francis enjoyed a cosmopolitan education, attending
schools in Italy, America, Germany, and England, and he was
competent in many languages. During the American Victorian
age, this genteel education and lifestyle were held in the highest
esteem, and Crawford's novels were particularly popular as the
twentieth century approached. He believed that stories should
provide pure entertainment, and as a born storyteller, he needn't
turn to the writer's method of expressing mankind's dilemmas or
taking social and political stands. Despite his popularity a
century ago, Crawford is barely read today, and what remains
to his name are his short ghost stories, written for literary
magazines that would provide quick cash and a bit of public
relations for his novels. "For the Blood Is the Life," "The Upper
Berth," and "The Screaming Skull" are not representative of his
work as a whole, not in style, length, or topic, yet they are
readily anthologized as a celebration of the man's literary craft.
For *One Dark Night*, I chose a story that is virtually unknown,
"The Dead Smile." Crawford's cunning haunting of this young
couple will give you the chills.

Sir Hugh Ockram smiled as he sat by the open window of his study, in the late August afternoon, and just then a curiously yellow cloud obscured the low sun, and the clear summer light turned lurid, as if it had been suddenly poisoned and polluted by the foul vapors of a plague. Sir Hugh's face seemed, at best, to be made of fine parchment drawn skintight over a wooden mask, in which two eyes were sunk out of sight, and peered from far within through crevices under the slanting, wrinkled lids, alive and watchful like two toads in their holes, side by side and exactly alike. But as the light changed, then a yellow glare flashed in each. Nurse Macdonald said once that when Sir Hugh smiled he saw the faces of two women in hell—two dead women he had betrayed. (Nurse Macdonald was a hundred years old.) And the smile widened, stretching the pale lips across the discolored teeth in an expression of profound self-satisfaction, blended with the most unforgiving hatred and contempt for the human doll. The hideous disease of which he was dying had touched his brain. His son stood beside him, tall, white, and delicate as an angel in a primitive picture, and though there was deep distress in his violet eyes as he looked at his father's face, he felt the shadow of that sickening smile stealing across his own lips and parting them and drawing them against his will.

And it was like a bad dream, for he tried not to smile and smiled the more. Beside him, strangely like him in her wan, angelic beauty, with the same shadowy golden hair, the same sad violet eyes, the same luminously pale face, Evelyn Warburton rested one hand upon his arm. And as she looked into her uncle's eyes, and could not turn her own away, she knew that the deathly smile was hovering on her own red lips, drawing them tightly across her little teeth, while two bright tears ran down her cheeks to her mouth, and dropped from the upper to the lower lip while she smiled—and the smile was like the shadow of death and the seal of damnation upon her pure, young face.

"Of course," said Sir Hugh very slowly, and still looking out at the trees, "if you have made up your mind to be married, I cannot hinder you, and I don't suppose you attach the smallest importance to my consent—"

"Father!" exclaimed Gabriel reproachfully.

"No, I do not deceive myself," continued the old man, smiling terribly. "You will marry when I am dead, though there is a very good reason why you had better not—why you had better not," he repeated very emphatically, and he slowly turned his toad eyes upon the lovers.

"What reason?" asked Evelyn in a frightened voice.

"Never mind the reason, my dear. You will marry just as if it did not exist." There was a long pause. "Two gone," he said, his voice lowering strangely, "and two more will be four—all together—forever and ever, burning, burning, burning bright."

At the last words his head sank slowly back, and the little glare of the toad eyes disappeared under the swollen lids, and the lurid cloud passed from the westering sun, so that the earth was green again and the light pure. Sir Hugh had fallen asleep, as he often did in his last illness, even while speaking.

Gabriel Ockram drew Evelyn away, and from the study they went out into the dim hall, softly closing the door behind them, and each audibly drew breath, as though some sudden danger had been passed. They laid their hands each in the other's, and their strangely alike eyes met in a long look, in which love and perfect understanding were darkened by the secret terror of an unknown thing. Their pale faces reflected each other's fear.

"It is his secret," said Evelyn at last. "He will never tell us what it is."

"If he died with it," answered Gabriel, "let it be on his own head!"

"On his head!" echoed the dim hall. It was a strange echo, and some were frightened by it, for they said that if it were a real echo it should repeat everything and not give back a phrase here and there, now speaking, now silent. But Nurse Macdonald said that the great hall would never echo a prayer when an Ockram was to die, though it would give back curses ten for one.

"On his head!" it repeated quite softly, and Evelyn started and looked round.

"It is only the echo," said Gabriel, leading her away.

They went out into the late afternoon light, and sat upon a stone seat behind the chapel, which was built across the end of the east wing. It was very still, not a breath stirred, and there was no sound near them. Only far off in the park a songbird was whistling the high prelude to the evening chorus.

"It is very lonely here," said Evelyn, taking Gabriel's hand nervously, and speaking as if she dreaded to disturb the silence. "If it were dark, I should be afraid."

"Of what? Of me?" Gabriel's sad eyes turned to her.

"Oh no! How could I be afraid of you? But of the old Ockrams—they say they are just under our feet here in the north vault outside the chapel, all in their shrouds, with no coffins, as they used to bury them."

"As they always will—as they will bury my father, and me. They say an Ockram will not lie in a coffin."

"But it cannot be true—these are fairy tales—ghost stories!" Evelyn nestled nearer to her companion, grasping his hand more tightly, and the sun began to go down.

"Of course. But there is a story of old Sir Vernon, who was beheaded for treason under James II. The family brought his body back from the scaffold in an iron coffin with heavy locks, and they put it in the north vault. But ever afterwards, whenever the vault was opened to bury another of the family, they found the coffin wide open, and the body standing upright against the wall, and the head rolled away in a corner, smiling at it."

"As Uncle Hugh smiles?" Evelyn shivered.

"Yes. I shall see him laid there too—with his secret, whatever it is." Gabriel sighed and pressed the girl's little hand.

"I do not like to think of it," she said unsteadily. "O Gabriel, what can the secret be? He said we had better not marry—not that he forbade it—but he said it so strangely, and he smiled—ugh!" Her small white teeth chattered with fear, and she looked over her shoulder while drawing still closer to Gabriel. "And, somehow, I felt it in my own face—"

"So did I," answered Gabriel in a low, nervous voice. "Nurse Macdonald—" He stopped abruptly.

"What? What did she say?"

"Oh—nothing. She has told me things—they would frighten you, dear. Come, it is growing chilly." He rose, but Evelyn held his hand in both of hers, still sitting and looking up into his face.

"But we shall be married, just the same—Gabriel! Say that we shall!"

"Of course, darling—of course. But while my father is so very ill, it is impossible—"

"O Gabriel, Gabriel dear! I wish we were married now!" cried Evelyn in sudden distress. "I know that something will prevent it and keep us apart."

"Nothing shall!"

"Nothing?"

"Nothing human," said Gabriel Ockram, as she drew him down to her.

And their faces, that were so strangely alike, met and touched—and Gabriel knew that the kiss had a marvelous savor of evil, but on Evelyn's lips it was like the cool breath of a sweet and mortal fear. And neither of them understood, for they were innocent and young. Yet she drew him to her by her lightest touch, as a sensitive plant shivers and waves its thin leaves, and bends and closes softly upon what it wants, and he let himself be drawn to her willingly, as he would if her touch had been deadly and poisonous; for she strangely loved that half-voluptuous breath of fear, and he passionately desired the nameless evil something that lurked in her maiden lips.

"It is as if we loved in a strange dream," she said.

"I fear the waking," he murmured.

"We shall not wake, dear—when the dream is over it will have already turned into death, so softly that we shall not know it. But until then—"

She paused, and her eyes sought his, and their faces slowly came nearer. It was as if they had thoughts in their red lips that foresaw and foreknew the deep kiss of each other.

"Until then—" she said again, very low, and her mouth was nearer to his.

"Dream—till then," murmured his breath.

II

Nurse Macdonald was a hundred years old. She used to sleep sitting all bent together in a great old leathern armchair with wings, her feet in a bag footstool lined with sheepskin, and many warm blankets wrapped about her, even in summer. Beside her a little lamp always burned at night by an old silver cup, in which there was something to drink.

Her face was very wrinkled, but the wrinkles were so small and fine and near together that they made shadows instead of lines. Two thin locks of hair, that was turning from white to a smoky yellow again, were drawn over her temples from under her starched white cap. Every now and then she woke, and her eyelids were drawn up in tiny folds like little pink silk curtains, and her queer blue eyes looked straight before her through doors and walls and worlds to a far place beyond. Then she slept again, and her hands lay one upon the other on the edge of the blanket, the thumbs had grown longer than the fingers with age, and the joints shone in the low lamplight like polished crabapples.

It was nearly one o'clock in the night, and the summer breeze was blowing the ivy branch against the panes of the window with a hushing caress. In the small room beyond, with the door ajar, the girl-maid who took care of Nurse Macdonald was fast asleep. All was very quiet. The old woman breathed regularly, and her eyes were shut.

But outside the closed window there was a face, and violet eyes were looking steadily at the ancient sleeper, for it was like the face of Evelyn Warburton, though there were eighty feet from the sill of the window to the foot of the tower. Yet the cheeks were thinner than Evelyn's, and as white as a gleam, and her eyes stared, and the lips were not red with life, they were dead and painted with new blood.

Slowly Nurse Macdonald's wrinkled eyelids folded themselves back, and she looked straight at the face at the window while one might count ten.

"Is it time?" she asked in her little old, faraway voice.

While she looked the face at the window changed, for the eyes opened wider and wider till the white glared all around the bright violet, and the bloody lips opened over gleaming teeth, and stretched and widened and stretched again, and the shadow golden hair rose and streamed against the window in the night breeze. And in answer to Nurse Macdonald's question came the sound that freezes the living flesh.

That low moaning voice that rises suddenly, like the scream of storm, from a moan to a wail, from a wail to a howl, from a howl to the fear-shriek of the tortured dead—he who has heard knows, and he can bear witness that the cry of the banshee is an evil cry to hear alone in the deep night. When it was over and the face was gone, Nurse Macdonald shook a little in her great chair, and still she looked at the black square of the window, but there was nothing more there, nothing but the night, and the whispering ivy branch. She turned her head to the door that was ajar, and there stood the girl in her white gown, her teeth chattering with fright.

"It is time, child," said Nurse Macdonald. "I must go to him, for it is the end."

She rose slowly, leaning her withered hands upon the arms of the chair, and the girl brought her a woolen gown and a great mantle, and her crutch-stick, and made her ready. But very often the girl looked at the window and was unjointed with fear and often Nurse Macdonald shook her head and said words which the maid could not understand.

"It was like the face of Miss Evelyn," said the girl at last, trembling.

But the ancient woman looked up sharply and angrily, and her queer blue eyes glared. She held herself by the arm of the great chair with her left hand, and lifted up her crutch-stick to strike the maid with all her might. But she did not.

"You are a good girl," she said, "but you are a fool. Pray for wit, child, pray for wit—or else find service in another house than Ockram Hall. Bring the lamp and help me under my left arm."

The crutch-stick clacked on the wooden floor, and the low heels of the woman's slippers clappered after her in slow triplets, as Nurse Macdonald got toward the door. And down the stairs each step she took was a

labor in itself, and by the clacking noise the waking servants knew that she was coming, very long before they
saw her.

No one was sleeping now, and there were lights
and whisperings and pale faces in the corridors near Sir
Hugh's bedroom, and now someone went in, and now
someone came out, but everyone made way for Nurse
Macdonald, who had nursed Sir Hugh's father more than
eighty years ago.

The light was soft and clear in the room. There stood
Gabriel Ockram by his father's bedside, and there knelt
Evelyn Warburton, her hair lying like a golden shadow
down her shoulders, and her hands clasped nervously together. And opposite Gabriel, a nurse was trying to make
Sir Hugh drink. But he would not, and though his lips
were parted, his teeth were set. He was very, very thin
and yellow now, and his eyes caught the light sideways
and were as yellow coals.

"Do not torment him," said Nurse Macdonald to the
woman who held the cup. "Let me speak to him, for his
hour is come."

"Let her speak to him," said Gabriel in a dull voice.

So the ancient woman leaned to the pillow and laid
the featherweight of her withered hand, that was like a
brown moth, upon Sir Hugh's yellow fingers, and she
spoke to him earnestly, while only Gabriel and Evelyn
were left in the room to hear.

"Hugh Ockram," she said, "this is the end of your life;
and as I saw you born, and saw your father born before
you, I am come to see you die. Hugh Ockram, will you
tell me the truth?"

The dying man recognized the little faraway voice
he had known all his life, and he very slowly turned his

yellow face to Nurse Macdonald; but he said nothing. Then she spoke again.

"Hugh Ockram, you will never see the daylight again. Will you tell the truth?"

His toadlike eyes were not dull yet. They fastened themselves on her face.

"What do you want of me?" he asked, and each word struck hollow on the last. "I have no secrets. I have lived a good life."

Nurse Macdonald laughed—a tiny, cracked laugh, that made her old head bob and tremble a little, as if her neck were on a steel spring. But Sir Hugh's eyes grew red, and his pale lips began to twist.

"Let me die in peace," he said slowly.

But Nurse Macdonald shook her head, and her brown, mothlike hand left his and fluttered to his forehead.

"By the mother that bore you and died of grief for the sins you did, tell me the truth!"

Sir Hugh's lips tightened on his discolored teeth.

"Not on earth," he answered slowly.

"By the wife who bore your son and died heart-broken, tell me the truth!"

"Neither to you in life, nor to her in eternal death."

His lips writhed, as if the words were coals between them, and a great drop of sweat rolled across the parchment of his forehead. Gabriel Ockram bit his hand as he watched his father die. But Nurse Macdonald spoke a third time.

"By the woman whom you betrayed, and who waits for you this night, Hugh Ockram, tell me the truth!"

"It is too late. Let me die in peace."

The writhing lips began to smile across the set yellow teeth, and the toad eyes glowed like evil jewels in his head.

"There is time," said the ancient woman. "Tell me the name of Evelyn Warburton's father. Then I will let you die in peace."

Evelyn started back, kneeling as she was, and stared at Nurse Macdonald, and then at her uncle.

"The name of Evelyn's father?" he repeated slowly, while the awful smile spread upon his dying face.

The light was growing strangely dim in the great room. As Evelyn looked, Nurse Macdonald's crooked shadow on the wall grew gigantic. Sir Hugh's breath came thick, rattling in his throat, as death crept in like a snake and choked it back. Evelyn prayed aloud, high and clear.

Then something rapped at the window, and she felt her hair rise upon her head in a cool breeze, as she looked around in spite of herself. And when she saw her own white face looking in at the window, and her own eyes staring at her through the glass, wise and fearful, and her own hair streaming against the pane, and her own lips dashed with blood, she rose slowly from the floor and stood rigid for one moment, till she screamed once and fell straight back into Gabriel's arms. But the shriek that answered hers was the fear-shriek of the tormented corpse, out of which the soul cannot pass for shame of deadly sins, though the devils fight in it with corruption, each for their due share.

Sir Hugh Ockram sat upright in his deathbed, and saw and cried aloud:

"Evelyn!" His harsh voice broke and rattled in his chest as he sank down. But still Nurse Macdonald tortured him, for there was a little life left in him still.

"You have seen the mother as she waits for you, Hugh Ockram. Who was this girl Evelyn's father? What was his name?"

For the last time the dreadful smile came upon the twisted lips, very slowly, very surely now, and the toad eyes glared red, and the parchment face glowed a little in the flickering light. For the last time words came.

"They know it in hell."

Then the glowing eyes went out quickly, the yellow face turned waxen pale, and a great shiver ran through the thin body as Hugh Ockram died.

But in death he still smiled, for he knew his secret and kept it still, on the other side, and he would take it with him, to lie with him forever in the north vault of the chapel where the Ockrams lie uncoffined in their shrouds—all but one. Though he was dead, he smiled, for he had kept his treasure of evil truth to the end, and there was none left to tell the name he had spoken, but there was all the evil he had not undone left to bear fruit.

As they watched—Nurse Macdonald and Gabriel, who held Evelyn still unconscious in his arms while he looked at the father—they felt the dead smile crawling along their own lips—the ancient crone and the youth with the angel's face. Then they shivered a little, and both looked at Evelyn as she lay with her head on his shoulder, and, though she was very beautiful, the same sickening smile was twisting her young mouth too, and it was like the foreshadowing of a great evil which they could not understand.

But by and by they carried Evelyn out, and she opened her eyes and the smile was gone. From far away

in the great house the sound of weeping and crooning
came up the stairs and echoed along the dismal corridors,
for the women had begun to mourn the dead master, after the Irish fashion, and the hall had echoes of its own
all that night, like the far-off wail of the banshee among
forest trees.

When the time was come they took Sir Hugh in his
winding-sheet on a trestle bier, and bore him to the
chapel and through the iron door and down the long descent to the north vault, with tapers, to lay him by his father. And two men went in first to prepare the place, and
came back staggering like drunken men, and white, leaving their lights behind them.

But Gabriel Ockram was not afraid, for he knew. And
he went in alone and saw that the body of Sir Vernon
Ockram was leaning upright against the stone wall, and
that his head lay on the ground nearby with the face
turned up, and the dried leathern lips smiled horribly
at the dried-up corpse, while the iron coffin, lined with
black velvet, stood open on the floor.

Then Gabriel took the thing in his hands, for it was
very light, being quite dried by the air of the vault, and
those who peeped in from the door saw him lay it in the
coffin again, and it rustled a little, like a bundle of reeds,
and sounded hollow as it touched the sides and the bottom. He also placed the head upon the shoulders and
shut down the lid, which fell to with a rusty spring that
snapped.

After that they laid Sir Hugh beside his father, with
the trestle bier on which they had brought him, and they
went back to the chapel.

But when they saw one another's faces, master and

men, they were all smiling with the dead smile of the corpse they had left in the vault, so that they could not bear to look at one another until it had faded away.

III

Gabriel Ockram became Sir Gabriel, inheriting the baronetcy with the half-ruined fortune left by his father, and still Evelyn Warburton lived at Ockram Hall, in the south room that had been hers ever since she could remember anything. She could not go away, for there were no relatives to whom she could have gone, and, besides, there seemed to be no reason why she should not stay. The world would never trouble itself to care what the Ockrams did on their Irish estates, and it was long since the Ockrams had asked anything of the world.

So Sir Gabriel took his father's place at the dark old table in the dining room, and Evelyn sat opposite to him, until such time as their mourning should be over, and they might be married at last. And meanwhile their lives went on as before, since Sir Hugh had been a hopeless invalid during the last year of his life, and they had seen him but once a day for the little while, spending most of their time together in a strangely perfect companionship.

But though the late summer saddened into autumn, and autumn darkened into winter, and storm followed storm, and rain poured on rain through the short days and the long nights, yet Ockram Hall seemed less gloomy since Sir Hugh had been laid in the north vault beside his father. And at Christmastide Evelyn decked the great hall with holly and green boughs, and huge fires blazed on every hearth. Then the tenants were all bidden to a New Year's dinner, and they ate and drank well, while Sir

Gabriel sat at the head of the table. Evelyn came in when the port wine was brought, and the most respected of the tenants made a speech to propose her health.

It was long, he said, since there had been a Lady Ockram. Sir Gabriel shaded his eyes with his hand and looked down at the table, but a faint color came into Evelyn's transparent cheeks. But, said the gray-haired farmer, it was longer still since there had been a Lady Ockram so fair as the next was to be, and he gave the health of Evelyn Warburton.

Then the tenants all stood up and shouted for her, and Sir Gabriel stood up likewise, beside Evelyn. And when the men gave the last and loudest cheer of all there was a voice not theirs, above them all, higher, fiercer, louder—a scream not earthly, shrieking for the bride of Ockram Hall. And the holly and the green boughs over the great chimneypiece shook and slowly waved as if a cool breeze were blowing over them. But the men turned very pale, and many of them set down their glasses, but others let them fall upon the floor for fear. And looking into one another's faces, they were all smiling strangely, a dead smile, like dead Sir Hugh's. One cried out words in Irish, and the fear of death was suddenly upon them all so that they fled in panic, falling over one another like wild beasts in the burning forest, when the thick smoke runs along before the flame, and the tables were overset, and drinking glasses and bottles were broken in heaps, and the dark red wine crawled like blood upon the polished floor.

Sir Gabriel and Evelyn stood alone at the head of the table before the wreck of the feast, not daring to turn to see each other, for each knew that the other smiled. But his right arm held her and his left hand clasped her right as they stared before them, and but for the shadows of her hair one might not have told their two faces apart. They listened long, but the cry came not again, and the dead smile faded from their lips, while each remembered that Sir Hugh Ockram lay in the north vault, smiling in his winding-sheet, in the dark, because he had died with his secret.

So ended the tenants' New Year's dinner. But from that time on Sir Gabriel grew more and more silent, and his face grew even paler and thinner than before. Often without warning and without words, he would rise from his seat, as if something moved him against his will, and he would go out into the rain or the sunshine to the north side of the chapel, and sit on the stone bench, staring at the ground as if he could see through it, and through the vault below, and through the white winding-sheet in the dark, to the dead smile that would not die.

Always when he went out in that way Evelyn came out presently and sat beside him. Once, too, as in summer, their beautiful faces came suddenly near, and their lids drooped, and their red lips were almost joined together. But as their eyes met, they grew wide and wild, so that the white showed in a ring all round the deep violet, and their teeth chattered, and their hands were like hands of corpses, each in the other's for the terror of what was under their feet, and of what they knew but could not see.

Once, also, Evelyn found Sir Gabriel in the chapel alone, standing before the iron door that led down to the place of death, and in his hand there was the key to the door, but he had not put it in the lock. Evelyn drew him away, shivering, for she had also been driven in waking dreams to see that terrible thing again, and to find out whether it had changed since it had lain there.

"I'm going mad," said Sir Gabriel, covering his eyes with his hand as he went with her. "I see it in my sleep, I see it when I am awake—it draws me to it, day and night—and unless I see it I shall die!"

"I know," answered Evelyn, "I know. It is as if threads were spun from it, like a spider's, drawing us down to it." She was silent for a moment, and then she started violently and grasped his arm with a man's strength, and almost screamed the words she spoke. "But we must not go there!" she cried. "We must not go!"

Sir Gabriel's eyes were half-shut, and he was not moved by the agony of her face.

"I shall die, unless I see it again," he said, in a quiet voice not like his own. And all that day and that evening he scarcely spoke, thinking of it, always thinking, while Evelyn Warburton quivered from head to foot with a terror she had never known.

She went alone, on a gray winter's morning, to Nurse Macdonald's room in the tower, and sat down beside the great leathern easy chair, laying her thin white hand upon the withered fingers.

"Nurse," she said, "what was it that Uncle Hugh should have told you, that night before he died? It must have been an awful secret—and yet, though you asked him, I feel somehow that you know it, and that you know why he used to smile so dreadfully."

The old woman's head moved slowly from side to side.

"I only guess—I shall never know," she answered slowly in her cracked little voice.

"But what do you guess? Who am I? Why did you ask who my father was? You know I am Colonel Warburton's daughter, and my mother was Lady Ockram's sister, so that Gabriel and I are cousins. My father was killed in Afghanistan. What secret can there be?"

"I do not know. I can only guess."

"Guess what?" asked Evelyn imploringly, and pressing the soft withered hands, as she leaned forward. But Nurse Macdonald's wrinkled lids dropped suddenly over her queer blue eyes, and her lips shook a little with her breath, as if she were asleep.

Evelyn waited. By the fire the Irish maid was knitting fast, and the needles clicked like three or four clocks ticking against each other. And the real clock on the wall solemnly ticked alone, checking off the seconds of the woman who was a hundred years old, and had not many days left. Outside the ivy branch beat the window in the wintry blast, as it had beaten against the glass a hundred years ago.

Then as Evelyn sat there she felt again the waking of a horrible desire—the sickening wish to go down, down to the thing in the north vault, and to open the winding-sheet, and see whether it had changed, and she held Nurse Macdonald's hands as if to keep herself in her place and fight against the appalling attraction of the evil dead.

But the old cat that kept Nurse Macdonald's feet warm, lying always on the bag footstool, got up and stretched itself, and looked up into Evelyn's eyes, while its back arched, and its tail thickened and bristled, and its ugly pink lips drew back in a devilish grin, showing its sharp teeth. Evelyn stared at it, half-fascinated by its ugliness. Then the creature suddenly put out one paw with all its claws spread, and spat at the girl, and all at once the grinning cat was like the smiling corpses far down below, so that Evelyn shivered down to her small feet and covered her face with her free hand lest Nurse Macdonald should wake and see the dead smile there, for she could feel it.

The old woman had already opened her eyes again, and she touched her cat with the end of her crutch-stick, whereupon its back went down and its tail shrunk, and it sidled back to its place on the bag footstool. But its yellow eyes looked up sideways at Evelyn, between the slits of its lids.

"What is it that you guess, nurse?" asked the young girl again.

"A bad thing—a wicked thing. But I dare not tell you, lest it might not be true, and the very thought should blast your life. For if I guess right, he meant that you should not know, and that you two should marry, and pay for his old sin with your souls."

"He used to tell us that we ought not to marry—"

"Yes—he told you that, perhaps—but it was as if a man put poisoned meat before a starving beast, and said do not eat but never raised his hand to take the meat away. And if he told you that you should not marry, it was because he hoped you would, for of all men living or dead, Hugh Ockram was the falsest man that ever told a cowardly lie, and the cruelest that ever hurt a weak woman, and the worst that ever loved a sin."

"But Gabriel and I love each other," said Evelyn very sadly.

Nurse Macdonald's old eyes looked far away, at sights seen long ago, and that rose in the gray winter air amid the mists of an ancient youth.

"If you love, you can die together," she said, very slowly. "Why should you live, if it is true? I am a hundred years old. What has life given me? The beginning is fire, the end is a heap of ashes, and between the end and the beginning lies all the pain in the world. Let me sleep, since I cannot die."

Then the old woman's eyes closed again, and her head sank a little lower upon her breast.

So Evelyn went away and left her asleep, with the cat asleep on the bag footstool; and the young girl tried to forget Nurse Macdonald's words, but she could not, for she heard them over and over again in the wind, and behind her on the stairs. And as she grew sick with fear of the frightful unknown evil to which her soul was bound, she felt a bodily something pressing her, and pushing her, and forcing her on, and from the other side she felt the threads that drew her mysteriously, and when she shut her eyes, she saw in the chapel behind the altar, the low iron door through which she must pass to go to the thing.

And as she lay awake at night, she drew the sheet over her face, lest she should see shadows on the wall beckoning her and the sound of her own warm breath made whisperings in her ears, while she held the mattress with her hands, to keep from getting up and going to the chapel. It would have been easier if there had not been a way thither through the library, by a door which was never locked. It would be fearfully easy to take her candle and go softly through the sleeping house. And the key of the vault lay under the altar behind a stone that turned. She knew the little secret. She could go alone and see.

But when she thought of it, she felt her hair rise on

her head, and first she shivered so that the bed shook, and then the horror went through her in a cold thrill that was agony again, like myriads of icy needles, boring into her nerves.

IV

The old clock in Nurse Macdonald's tower struck midnight. From her room she could hear the creaking chains and weights in their box in the corner of the staircase, and overhead the jarring of the rusty lever that lifted the hammer. She had heard it all her life. It struck eleven strokes clearly and then came the twelfth, with a dull half stroke, as though the hammer were too weary to go on, and had fallen asleep against the bell.

The old cat got up from the bag footstool and stretched itself, and Nurse Macdonald opened her ancient eyes and looked slowly round the room by the dim light of the night lamp. She touched the cat with her crutchstick, and it lay down upon her feet. She drank a few drops from her cup and went to sleep again.

But downstairs Sir Gabriel sat straight up as the clock struck, for he had dreamed a fearful dream of horror, and his heart stood still, till he awoke at its stopping, and it beat again furiously with his breath, like a wild thing set free. No Ockram had ever known fear waking, but sometimes it came to Sir Gabriel in his sleep.

He pressed his hands to his temples as he sat up in bed, and his hands were icy cold, but his head was hot. The dream faded far, and in its place there came the master thought that racked his life; with the thought also came the sick twisting of his lips in the dark that would have been a smile. Far off, Evelyn Warburton dreamed that the dead smile was on her mouth, and awoke, starting with a little moan, her face in her hands, shivering.

But Sir Gabriel struck a light and got up and began to walk up and down his great room. It was midnight, and he had barely slept an hour, and in the north of Ireland the winter nights are long.

"I shall go mad," he said to himself, holding his forehead. He knew that it was true. For weeks and months the possession of the thing had grown upon him like a disease, till he could think of nothing without thinking first of that. And now all at once it outgrew his strength, and he knew that he must be its instrument or lose his mind—that he must do the deed he hated and feared, if he could fear anything, or that something would snap in his brain and divide him from life while he was yet alive. He took the candlestick in his hand, the old-fashioned heavy candlestick that had always been used by the head of the house. He did not think of dressing, but went as he was, in his silk nightclothes and his slippers, and he opened the door. Everything was very still in the great old house. He shut the door behind him and walked noiselessly on the carpet through the long corridor. A cool breeze blew over his shoulder and blew the flame of his candle straight out from him. Instinctively he stopped and looked round, but all was still, and the upright flame burned steadily. He walked on, and instantly a strong draft was behind him, almost extinguishing the light. It seemed to blow him on his way, ceasing whenever he turned, coming again when he went on—invisible, icy.

Down the great staircase to the echoing hall he went, seeing nothing but the flaring flame of the candle standing away from him over the guttering wax, while the cold wind blew over his shoulder and through his hair. On he passed through the open door into the library, dark with old books and carved bookcases, on through the door in the shelves, with painted shelves on it, and the imitated backs of books, so that one needed to know where to find it—and it shut itself after him with a soft click. He entered the low-arched passage, and though the door was shut behind him and fitted tightly in its frame, still the cold breeze blew the flame forward as he walked. And he was not afraid, but his face was very pale, and his eyes were wise and bright, looking before him, seeing already in the dark air the picture of the thing beyond. But in the chapel he stood still, his hand on the little turning stone tablet in the back of the stone altar. On the tablet were engraved words, *"Clavis sepulchri Clarissimorum Dominorum De Ockram"*—("the key to the vault of the most illustrious lord of Ockram"). Sir Gabriel paused and listened. He fancied that he heard a sound far off in the great house where all had been so still, but it did not come again. Yet he waited at the last, and looked at the low iron door. Beyond it, down the long descent, lay his father uncoffined, six months dead, corrupt, terrible in his clinging shroud. The strangely preserving air of the vault could not yet have done its work completely. But on the thing's ghastly features, with their half-dried, open eyes, there would still be the frightful smile with which the man had died—the smile that haunted—

As the thought crossed Sir Gabriel's mind, he felt his lips writhing, and he struck his own mouth in wrath with the back of his hand so fiercely that a drop of blood ran down his chin and another, and more, falling back in the gloom upon the chapel pavement. But still his bruised lips twisted themselves. He turned the tablet by the simple secret. It needed no safer fastening, for had each Ockram been confined in pure gold, and had the door been wide, there was not a man in Tyrone brave enough to go down to the place, saving Gabriel Ockram himself, with his angel's face and his thin, white hands, and his sad unflinching eyes. He took the great gold key and set it into the lock of the iron door, and the heavy, rattling noise echoed down the descent beyond like footsteps, as if a watcher had stood behind the iron and were running away within, with heavy dead feet. And though he was standing still, the cool wind was from behind him, and blew the flame of the candle against the iron panel. He turned the key.

Sir Gabriel saw that his candle was short. There were new ones on the altar with long candlesticks and he lit one, and left his own burning on the floor. As he set it down on the pavement his lip began to bleed again, and another drop fell upon the stones.

He drew the iron door open and pushed it back against the chapel wall, so that it should not shut of itself, while he was within, and the horrible draft of the sepulchre came up out of the depths in his face, foul and dark. He went in, but though the fetid air met him, yet the flame of the tall candle was blown straight from him against the wind while he walked down the easy incline with steady steps, his loose slippers slapping the pavement as he trod.

He shaded the candle with his hand, and his fingers seemed to be made of wax and blood as the light shone through them. And in spite of him the unearthly draft forced the flame forward, till it was blue over the black wick, and it seemed as if it must go out. But he went straight on, with shining eyes.

The downward passage was wide, and he could not always see the walls by the struggling light, but he knew when he was in the place of death by the larger, drearier echo of his steps in the greater space and by the sensation of a distant blank wall. He stood still, almost enclosing the flame of the candle in the hollow of his hand. He could see a little, for his eyes were growing used to the gloom. Shadowy forms were outlined in the dimness, where the biers of the Ockrams stood crowded together, side by side, each with its straight, shrouded corpse, strangely preserved by the dry air, like the empty shell that the locust sheds in summer. And a few steps before him he saw clearly the dark shape of headless Sir Vernon's iron coffin, and he knew that nearest to it lay the thing he sought.

He was as brave as any of those dead men had been, and they were his fathers, and he knew that sooner or later he should lie there himself, beside Sir Hugh, slowly drying to a parchment shell. But he was still alive, and he closed his eyes a moment, and three great drops stood on his forehead.

Then he looked again, and by the whiteness of the winding-sheet he knew his father's corpse, for all the others were brown with age; and, moreover, the flame of the candle was blown toward it. He made four steps till he reached it, and suddenly the light burned straight and high, shedding a dazzling yellow glare upon the fine linen that was all white, save over the face, and where the joined hands were laid on the breast. And at those places ugly stains had spread, darkened with outlines of the features and of the tight-clasped fingers. There was a frightful stench of drying death.

As Sir Gabriel looked down, something stirred behind

him, softly at first, then more noisily, and something fell
to the stone floor with a dull thud and rolled up to his
feet; he started back, and saw a withered head lying almost face upward on the pavement, grinning at him. He
felt the cold sweat standing on his face, and his heart beat
painfully.

For the first time in all his life that evil thing which
men call fear was getting hold of him, checking his heart-
strings as a cruel driver checks a quivering horse, clawing
at his backbone with icy hands, lifting his hair with freez-
ing breath, climbing up and gathering in his midriff with
leaden weight.

Yet presently he bit his lip and bent down, holding
the candle in one hand, to lift the shroud back from the
head of the corpse with the other. Slowly he lifted it.
Then it clove to the half-dried skin of the face, and his
hand shook as if someone had struck him on the el-
bow, but half in fear and half in anger at himself, he pulled
it, so that it came away with a little ripping sound. He
caught his breath as he held it, not throwing it back, and
not yet looking. The horror was working on him, and he
felt that old Vernon Ockram was standing up in his iron
coffin, headless, yet watching him with the stump of his
severed neck.

While he held his breath he felt the dead smile twisting his lips. In sudden wrath at his own misery, he tossed
the death-stained linen backward, and looked at last. He
ground his teeth lest he should shriek aloud.

There it was, the thing that haunted him, that haunted
Evelyn Warburton, that was like a blight on all that came
near him.

The dead face was blotched with dark stains, and the
thin, gray hair was matted about the discolored forehead.

The sunken lids were half open, and the candlelight gleamed on something foul where the toad eyes had lived.

But yet the dead thing smiled, as it had smiled in life; the ghastly lips were parted and drawn wide and tight upon the wolfish teeth, cursing still, and still defying hell to do its worst—defying, cursing, and always and forever smiling alone in the dark.

Sir Gabriel opened the winding-sheet where the hands were, and the blackened, withered fingers were closed upon something stained and mottled. Shivering from head to foot, but fighting like a man in agony for his life, he tried to take the package from the dead man's hold. But as he pulled at it the clawlike fingers seemed to close more tightly, and when he pulled harder the shrunken hands and arms rose from the corpse with a horrible look of life following his motion—then as he wrenched the sealed packet loose at last, the hands fell back into their place still folded.

He set down the candle on the edge of the bier to break the seals from the stout paper. And, kneeling on one knee, to get a better light, he read what was within, written long ago in Sir Hugh's queer hand.

He was no longer afraid.

He read how Sir Hugh had written it all down that it might perchance be a witness of evil and of his hatred; how he had loved Evelyn Warburton, his wife's sister; and how his wife had died of a broken heart with his curse upon her, and how Warburton and he had fought side by side in Afghanistan, and Warburton had fallen; but Ockram had brought his comrade's wife back a full year later, and little Evelyn, her child, had been born in Ockram Hall. And next, how he had wearied of the mother, and she had died like her sister with his curse on her. And then, how Evelyn had been brought up as his niece, and how he had trusted that his son Gabriel and his daughter, innocent and unknowing, might love and marry, and the souls of the women he had betrayed might suffer another anguish before eternity was out. And, last of all, he hoped that someday, when nothing could be undone, the two might find his writing and live on, not daring to tell the truth for their children's sake and the world's word, man and wife.

This he read, kneeling beside the corpse in the north vault, by the light of the altar candle; and when he had read it all, he thanked God aloud that he had found the secret in time, but when he rose to his feet and looked down at the dead face it was changed, and the smile was gone from it forever, and the jaw had fallen a little, and the tired, dead lips were relaxed. And then there was a breath behind him and close to him, not cold like that which had blown the flame of the candle as he came, but warm and human. He turned suddenly.

There she stood, all in white, with her shadowy golden hair—for she had risen from her bed and had followed him noiselessly, and had found him reading, and had herself read over his shoulder. He started violently when he saw her, for his nerves were unstrung—and then he cried out her name in the still place of death:

"Evelyn!"

"My brother!" she answered, softly and tenderly, putting out both hands to meet his.

A Ghost Story

Mark Twain
(1835–1910)

If you have just finished Crawford's "The Dead Smile," no doubt
you are in need of some levity—and who better than Mark Twain
to deliver it! Considered internationally as a satirist and great
social philosopher, Samuel Clemens thought of himself as simply a
working journalist. He made it known that he wouldn't touch a
book unless it had potential—that is, in making money. Fortunately,
he had a knack for putting his finger right on the moral and ethical
pulse of the new America, values he shared and took to heart.
And he knew how to choose themes that would tickle the moral
fretwork of his readers, making his books quite marketable. A
Mississippi riverboat pilot before the Civil War, he once said that
he encountered all the types of human nature one met in
biography, history, or fiction right there on the river.
"A Ghost Story" is classic Twain: It economically and wittily
makes an observation about human nature, even in the afterlife.
The beginning will give you the creeps, but don't be afraid to read
it when the moon hangs high and the wind howls. The ghost, a
Cardiff Giant, whose origins, according to my scant sources, are
in Cardiff, the seaport of Glamorganshire in southeast Wales,
is a gentle and childlike sort who is in need of a helping hand
to find what is rightfully his.

I took a large room, far up Broadway, in a huge old building whose upper stories had been wholly unoccupied for years, until I came. The place had long been given up to dust and cobwebs, to solitude and silence. I seemed groping among the tombs and invading the privacy of the dead, that first night I climbed up to my quarters. For the first time in my life a superstitious dread came over me; and as I turned a dark angle of the stairway and an invisible cobweb swung its sleazy woof in my face and clung there, I shuddered as one who had encountered a phantom.

I was glad enough when I reached my room and locked out the mold and the darkness. A cheery fire was burning in the grate, and I sat down before it with a comforting sense of relief. For two hours I sat there, thinking of bygone times; recalling old scenes, and summoning half-forgotten faces out of the mists of the past; listening, in fancy, to voices that long ago grew silent for all time, and to once familiar songs that nobody sings now. And as my reverie softened down to a sadder and sadder pathos, the shrieking of the winds outside softened to a wail, the angry beating of the rain against the panes diminished to a tranquil patter, and one by one the noises in the street subsided, until the hurrying footsteps of the

last belated straggler died away in the distance and left
no sound behind.

The fire had burned low. A sense of loneliness crept
over me. I arose and undressed, moving on tiptoe about
the room, doing stealthily what I had to do, as if I were
environed by sleeping enemies whose slumbers it would
be fatal to break. I covered up in bed, and lay listening to
the rain and wind and the faint creaking of distant shutters, till they lulled me to sleep.

I slept profoundly, but how long I do not know. All
at once I found myself awake, and filled with a shuddering expectancy. All was still. All but my own heart—
I could hear it beat. Presently the bedclothes began to
slip away slowly toward the foot of the bed, as if someone were pulling them! I could not stir; I could not speak.
Still the blankets slipped deliberately away, till my breast
was uncovered. Then with a great effort I seized them
and drew them over my head. I waited, listened, waited.
Once more that steady pull began, and once more I lay
torpid a century of dragging seconds till my breast was
naked again. At last I roused my energies and snatched
the covers back to their place and held them with a
strong grip. I waited. By and by I felt a faint tug, and took
a fresh grip. The tug strengthened to a steady strain—it
grew stronger and stronger. My hold parted, and for the
third time the blankets slid away. I groaned. An answer-
ing groan came from the foot of the bed! Beaded drops
of sweat stood upon my forehead. I was more dead than
alive. Presently I heard a heavy footstep in my room—the
step of an elephant, it seemed to me—it was not like anything human. But it was moving FROM me—there was
relief in that. I heard it approach the door—pass out
without moving bolt or lock—and wander away among

the dismal corridors, straining the floors and joists till they creaked again as it passed—and then silence reigned once more.

When my excitement had calmed, I said to myself, "This is a dream—simply a hideous dream." And so I lay thinking it over until I convinced myself that it WAS a dream, and then a comforting laugh relaxed my lips and I was happy again. I got up and struck a light; and when I found that the locks and bolts were just as I had left them, another soothing laugh welled in my heart and rippled from my lips. I took my pipe and lit it, and was just sitting down before the fire, when—down went the pipe out of my nerveless fingers, the blood forsook my cheeks, and my placid breathing was cut short with a gasp! In the ashes on the hearth, side by side with my own bare footprint, was another, so vast that in comparison mine was but an infant's! Then I HAD had a visitor, and the elephant tread was explained.

I put out the light and returned to bed, palsied with fear. I lay a long time, peering into the darkness, and listening. Then I heard a grating noise overhead, like the dragging of a heavy body across the floor; then the throwing down of the body, and the shaking of my windows in response to the concussion. In distant parts of the building I heard the muffled slamming of doors. I heard, at intervals, stealthy footsteps creeping in and out among the corridors, and up and down the stairs. Sometimes these noises approached my door, hesitated, and went away again. I heard the clanking of chains faintly, in remote passages, and listened while the clanking grew nearer—while it wearily climbed the stairways, marking each move by the loose surplus of chain that fell with an accented rattle upon each succeeding step as the goblin that bore it advanced. I heard muttered sentences; half-uttered screams that seemed smothered violently; and the swish of invisible garments, the rush of invisible wings. Then I became conscious that my chamber was invaded—that I was not alone. I heard sighs and breathings about my bed, and mysterious whisperings. Three little spheres of soft phosphorescent light appeared on the ceiling directly over my head, clung and glowed there a moment, and then dropped—two of them upon my face and one upon the pillow. They spattered, liquidly, and felt warm. Intuition told me they had turned to gouts of blood as they fell—I needed no light to satisfy myself of that. Then I saw pallid faces, dimly luminous, and white uplifted hands, floating bodiless in the air—floating a moment and then disappearing. The whispering ceased, and the voices and the sounds, and a solemn stillness followed. I waited and listened. I felt that I must have light or die. I was weak with fear. I slowly raised myself toward a sitting posture, and my face came in contact with a clammy hand! All strength went from me apparently, and I fell back like a stricken invalid. Then I heard the rustle of a garment—it seemed to pass to the door and go out.

When everything was still once more, I crept out of bed, sick and feeble, and lit the gas with a hand that trembled as if it were aged with a hundred years. The light brought some little cheer to my spirits. I sat down and fell into a dreamy contemplation of that great footprint in the ashes. By and by its outlines began to waver and grow dim. I glanced up and the broad gas flame was slowly wilting away. In the same moment I heard that elephantine tread again. I noted its approach, nearer and nearer, along the musty halls, and dimmer and dimmer the light waned. The tread reached my very door and paused—the light had dwindled to a sickly blue, and all things about me lay in a spectral twilight. The door did not open, and yet I felt a faint gust of air fan my cheek, and presently was conscious of a huge, cloudy presence before me. I watched it with fascinated eyes. A pale glow stole over the Thing. Gradually its cloudy folds took shape— an arm appeared, then legs, then a body, and last a great sad face looked out of the vapor. Stripped of its filmy housings, naked, muscular and comely, the majestic Cardiff Giant loomed above me!

All my misery vanished—for a child might know that no harm could come with that benignant countenance. My cheerful spirits returned at once, and in sympathy with them the gas flamed up brightly again. Never a lonely outcast was so glad to welcome company as I was to greet the friendly giant. I said:

"Why, is it nobody but you? Do you know, I have been scared to death for the last two or three hours? I am most honestly glad to see you. I wish I had a chair— Here, here, don't try to sit down in that thing!"

But it was too late. He was in it before I could stop him, and down he went—I never saw a chair shivered so in my life.

"Stop, stop. You'll ruin ev—"

Too late again. There was another crash, and another chair was resolved into its original elements.

"Confound it, haven't you got any judgment at all? Do you want to ruin all the furniture on the place? Here, here, you petrified fool—"

But it was no use. Before I could arrest him he had sat down on the bed, and it was a melancholy ruin.

"Now what sort of a way is that to do? First you come lumbering about the place bringing a legion of vagabond goblins along with you to worry me to death, and then when I overlook an indelicacy of costume which would not be tolerated anywhere by cultivated people except in a respectable theater, and not even there if the nudity were of YOUR sex, you repay me by wrecking all the furniture you can find to sit down on. And why will you? You damage yourself as much as you do me. You have broken off the end of your spinal column, and littered up the floor with chips of your hams till the place looks like a marble yard. You ought to be ashamed of yourself—you are big enough to know better."

"Well, I will not break any more furniture. But what am I to do? I have not had a chance to sit down for a century." And the tears came into his eyes.

"Poor devil," I said, "I should not have been so harsh with you. And you are an orphan, too, no doubt. But sit down on the floor here—nothing else can stand your weight—and besides, we cannot be sociable with you away up there above me; I want you down where I can perch on this high counting-house stool and gossip with you face to face."

So he sat down on the floor, and lit a pipe which I gave him, threw one of my red blankets over his shoulders, inverted my sitz-bath on his head, helmet fashion, and made himself picturesque and comfortable. Then he crossed his ankles, while I renewed the fire, and exposed the flat, honey-combed bottoms of his prodigious feet to the grateful warmth.

"What is the matter with the bottom of your feet and the back of your legs, that they are gouged up so?"

"Infernal chilblains—I caught them clear up to the back of my head, roosting out there under Newell's farm. But I love the place; I love it as one loves his old home.

There is no peace for me like the peace I feel when I am there."

We talked along for half an hour, and then I noticed that he looked tired, and spoke of it. "Tired?" he said. "Well, I should think so. And now I will tell you all about it, since you have treated me so well. I am the spirit of the Petrified Man that lies across the street there in the museum. I am the ghost of the Cardiff Giant. I can have no rest, no peace, till they have given that poor body burial again. Now what was the most natural thing for me to do, to make men satisfy this wish? Terrify them into it!—haunt the place where the body lay! So I haunted the museum night after night. I even got other spirits to help me. But it did no good, for nobody ever came to the museum at midnight. Then it occurred to me to come over the way and haunt this place a little. I felt that if I ever got a hearing I must succeed, for I had the most efficient company that perdition could furnish. Night after night we have shivered around through these mildewed halls, dragging chains, groaning, whispering, tramping up and down stairs, till, to tell you the truth, I am almost worn out. But when I saw a light in your room tonight I roused my energies again and went at it with a deal of the old freshness. But I am tired out—entirely fagged out. Give me, I beseech you, give me some hope!"

I lit off my perch in a burst of excitement, and exclaimed:

"This transcends everything—everything that ever did occur! Why you poor blundering old fossil, you have had all your trouble for nothing—you have been haunting a PLASTER CAST of yourself—the real Cardiff Giant is in Albany!"

[Footnote by Twain: A fact. The original fraud was

ingeniously and fraudfully duplicated, and exhibited in New York as the "only genuine" Cardiff Giant (to the unspeakable disgust of the owners of the real colossus) at the very same time that the latter was drawing crowds at a museum in Albany.]

"Confound it, don't you know your own remains?"

I never saw such an eloquent look of shame, of pitiable humiliation, overspread a countenance before.

The Petrified Man rose slowly to his feet, and said:

"Honestly, IS that true?"

"As true as I am sitting here."

He took the pipe from his mouth and laid it on the mantel, then stood irresolute a moment (unconsciously, from old habit, thrusting his hands where his pantaloons pockets should have been, and meditatively dropping his chin on his breast), and finally said:

"Well—I NEVER felt so absurd before. The Petrified Man has sold everybody else, and now the mean fraud has ended by selling its own ghost! My son, if there is any charity left in your heart for a poor friendless phantom like me, don't let this get out. Think how YOU would feel if you had made such an ass of yourself."

I heard his stately tramp die away, step by step down the stairs and out into the deserted street, and felt sorry that he was gone, poor fellow—and sorrier still that he had carried off my red blanket and my bathtub.

The Judge's House

Bram Stoker
(1847–1912)

It's hard to believe, but *Dracula* never made much money for its creator. Bram Stoker, born in Clantarf (north of Dublin), always held a steady position: first as a civil servant; next as a junior clerk in the Dublin castle; and then as manager of the London Lyceum Theatre, which was owned by his longtime friend, actor Henry Irving. It was after 1905, when Irving died, that Stoker had to rely on his writing for income, but his themes of nightmare, curses, and horror entangled with romance brought mixed reviews. Some critics found his detailed descriptions repulsive. His short stories, written earlier in his career, and his romance novel, *The Snake's Pass*, were better received. His writing career as a whole was a landmark of horror literature; he became fixated with the boundaries of life and death. It is said that "The Judge's House" was part of Stoker's original *Dracula* manuscript.

*W*hen the time for his examination drew near Malcolm Malcolmson made up his mind to go somewhere to read by himself. He feared the attractions of the seaside, and also he feared completely rural isolation, for of old he knew its charms, and so he determined to find some unpretentious little town where there would be nothing to distract him. He refrained from asking suggestions from any of his friends, for he argued that each would recommend some place of which he had knowledge, and where he had already acquaintances. As Malcolmson wished to avoid friends he had no wish to encumber himself with the attention of friends' friends, and so he determined to look out for a place for himself. He packed a portmanteau with some clothes and all the books he required, and then took ticket for the first name on the local timetable which he did not know.

When at the end of three hours' journey he alighted at Benchurch, he felt satisfied that he had so far obliterated his tracks as to be sure of having a peaceful opportunity of pursuing his studies. He went straight to the one inn which the sleepy little place contained, and put up for the night. Benchurch was a market town, and once in three weeks was crowded to excess, but for the remainder of the twenty-one days it was as attractive as a desert.

Malcolmson looked around the day after his arrival to try to find quarters more isolated than even so quiet an inn as "The Good Traveller" afforded. There was only one place which took his fancy, and it certainly satisfied his wildest ideas regarding quiet. In fact, quiet was not the proper word to apply to it—desolation was the only term conveying any suitable idea of its isolation. It was an old rambling, heavy-built house of the Jacobean style, with heavy gables and windows, unusually small, and set higher than was customary in such houses, and was surrounded with a high brick wall massively built. Indeed, on examination, it looked more like a fortified house than an ordinary dwelling. But all these things pleased Malcolmson. "Here," he thought, "is the very spot I have been looking for, and if I can only get opportunity of using it I shall be happy." His joy was increased when he realized beyond doubt that it was not at present inhabited.

From the post office he got the name of the agent, who was rarely surprised at the application to rent a part of the old house. Mr. Carnford, the local lawyer and agent, was a genial old gentleman, and frankly confessed his delight at anyone being willing to live in the house.

"To tell you the truth," said he, "I should be only too happy, on behalf of the owners, to let anyone have the house rent free for a term of years if only to accustom the people here to see it inhabited. It has been so long empty that some kind of absurd prejudice has grown up about it, and this can be best put down by its occupation—if only," he added with a sly glance at Malcolmson, "by a scholar like yourself, who wants its quiet for a time."

Malcolmson thought it needless to ask the agent about the "absurd prejudice"; he knew he would get

more information, if he should require it, on that subject
from other quarters. He paid his three months' rent, got
a receipt and the name of an old woman who would
probably undertake to "do" for him, and came away with
the keys in his pocket. He then went to the landlady of
the inn, who was a cheerful and most kindly person, and
asked her advice as to such stores and provisions as he
would be likely to require. She threw up her hands in
amazement when he told her where he was going to settle himself.

"Not in the Judge's House!" she said, and grew pale
as she spoke. He explained the locality of the house, saying that he did not know its name. When he had finished
she answered:

"Aye, sure enough—sure enough the very place! It
is the Judge's House sure enough." He asked her to tell
him about the place, why so called, and what there was
against it. She told him that it was so called locally because it had been many years before—how long she
could not say, as she was herself from another part of the
country, but she thought it must have been a hundred
years or more—the abode of a judge who was held in
great terror on account of his harsh sentences and his
hostility to prisoners at Assizes. As to what there was
against the house itself she could not tell. She had often
asked, but no one could inform her; but there was a general feeling that there was something, and for her own
part she would not take all the money in Drinkwater's
Bank and stay in the house an hour by herself. Then she
apologized to Malcolmson for her disturbing talk.

"It is too bad of me, sir, and you—and a young
gentleman, too—if you will pardon me saying it, going to
live there all alone. If you were my boy—and you'll

excuse me for saying it—you wouldn't sleep there a night, not if I had to go there myself and pull the big alarm bell that's on the roof!" The good creature was so manifestly in earnest, and was so kindly in her intentions, that Malcolmson, although amused, was touched. He told her kindly how much he appreciated her interest in him, and added:

"But, my dear Mrs. Witham, indeed you need not be concerned about me! A man who is reading for the Mathematical Tripos has too much to think of to be disturbed by any of these mysterious 'somethings,' and his work is of too exact and prosaic a kind to allow of his having any corner in his mind for mysteries of any kind. Harmonical Progression, Permutations and Combinations, and Elliptic Functions have sufficient mysteries for me!" Mrs. Witham kindly undertook to see after his commissions, and he went himself to look for the old woman who had been recommended to him. When he returned to the Judge's House with her, after an interval of a couple of hours, he found Mrs. Witham herself waiting with several men and boys carrying parcels, and an upholsterer's man with a bed in a cart, for she said, though tables and chairs might be all very well, a bed that hadn't been aired for mayhap fifty years was not proper for young bones to lie on. She was evidently curious to see the inside of the house; and though manifestly so afraid of the "somethings" that at the slightest sound she clutched on to Malcolmson, whom she never left for a moment, went over the whole place.

After his examination of the house, Malcolmson decided to take up his abode in the great dining room, which was big enough to serve for all his requirements; and Mrs. Witham, with the aid of the charwoman, Mrs. Dempster, proceeded to arrange matters. When the hampers were brought in and unpacked, Malcolmson saw that with much kind forethought she had sent from her own kitchen sufficient provisions to last for a few days. Before going she expressed all sorts of kind wishes; and at the door turned and said:

"And perhaps, sir, as the room is big and drafty it might be well to have one of those big screens put around your bed at night—though, truth to tell, I would die myself if I were to be so shut in with all kinds of—of 'things,' that put their heads round the sides, or over the top, and look on me!" The image which she had called up was too much for her nerves, and she fled incontinently.

Mrs. Dempster sniffed in a superior manner as the landlady disappeared, and remarked that for her own part she wasn't afraid of all the bogies in the kingdom.

"I'll tell you what it is, sir," she said; "bogies is all kinds and sorts of things—except bogies! Rats and mice, and beetles; and creaky doors, and loose slates, and broken panes, and stiff drawer handles, that stay out when you pull them and then fall down in the middle of the night. Look at the wainscot of the room! It is old—hundreds of years old! Do you think there's no rats and beetles there! And do you imagine, sir, that you won't see none of them! Rats is bogies, I tell you, and bogies is rats; and don't you get to think anything else!"

"Mrs. Dempster," said Malcolmson gravely, making her a polite bow, "you know more than a Senior Wrangler! And let me say, that, as a mark of esteem for your indubitable soundness of head and heart, I shall, when I go, give you possession of this house, and let you stay here by yourself for the last two months of my tenancy, for four weeks will serve my purpose."

"Thank you kindly, sir," she answered, "but I couldn't sleep away from home a night. I am in Greenhow's Charity, and if I slept a night away from my rooms I should lose all I have got to live on. The rules is very strict; and there's too many watching for a vacancy for me to run any risks in the matter. Only for that, sir, I'd gladly come here and attend on you altogether during your stay."

"My good woman," said Malcolmson hastily, "I have come here on purpose to obtain solitude; and believe me that I am grateful to the late Greenhow for having so organized his admirable charity—whatever it is—that I am perforce denied the opportunity of suffering from such a form of temptation! Saint Anthony himself could not be more rigid on the point!"

The old woman laughed harshly. "Ah, you young gentlemen," she said, "you don't fear for naught; and belike you'll get all the solitude you want here." She set to work with her cleaning; and by nightfall, when Malcolmson returned from his walk—he always had one of his books to study as he walked—he found the room swept and tidied, a fire burning in the old hearth, the lamp lit, and the table spread for supper with Mrs. Witham's excellent fare. "This is comfort, indeed," he said, as he rubbed his hands.

When he had finished his supper, and lifted the tray to the other end of the great oak dining table, he got out his books again, put fresh wood on the fire, trimmed his lamp, and set himself down to a spell of real hard work. He went on without pause till about eleven o'clock, when he knocked off for a bit to fix his fire and lamp, and to make himself a cup of tea. He had always been a tea-drinker, and during his college life had sat late at work and had taken tea late. The rest was a great luxury to him, and he enjoyed it with a sense of delicious, voluptuous ease. The renewed fire leaped and sparkled, and threw quaint shadows through the great old room; and as he sipped his hot tea he reveled in the sense of isolation from his kind. Then it was that he began to notice for the first time what a noise the rats were making.

"Surely," he thought, "they cannot have been at it all the time I was reading. Had they been, I must have noticed it!" Presently, when the noise increased, he satisfied himself that it was really new. It was evident that at first the rats had been frightened at the presence of a stranger, and the light of fire and lamp; but that as the time went on they had grown bolder and were now disporting themselves as was their wont.

How busy they were! and hark to the strange noises! Up and down behind the old wainscot, over the ceiling and under the floor they raced, and gnawed, and scratched! Malcolmson smiled to himself as he recalled to mind the saying of Mrs. Dempster, "Bogies is rats, and rats is bogies!" The tea began to have its effect of intellectual and nervous stimulus; he saw with joy another long spell of work to be done before the night was past, and in the sense of security which it gave him, he allowed himself the luxury of a good look round the room. He took his lamp in one hand, and went all around, wondering that so quaint and beautiful an old house had been so long neglected. The carving of the oak on the panels of the wainscot was fine, and on and round the doors and windows it was beautiful and of rare merit. There were some old pictures on the walls, but they were coated so thick with dust and dirt that he could not distinguish any detail of them, though he held his lamp as high as he could over his head. Here and there as he went round he saw some crack or hole blocked for a moment by the face of a rat with its bright eyes glittering in the light, but in an instant it was gone, and a squeak and a scamper followed.

The thing that most struck him, however, was the rope of the great alarm bell on the roof, which hung down in a corner of the room on the right-hand side of the fireplace. He pulled up close to the hearth a great high-backed carved oak chair, and sat down to his last cup of tea. When this was done he made up the fire, and went back to his work, sitting at the corner of the table, having the fire to his left. For a while the rats disturbed him somewhat with their perpetual scampering, but he got accustomed to the noise as one does to the ticking of a clock or to the roar of moving water; and he became so immersed in his work that everything in the world, except the problem which he was trying to solve, passed away from him.

He suddenly looked up, his problem was still unsolved, and there was in the air that sense of the hour before the dawn, which is so dread to doubtful life. The noise of the rats had ceased. Indeed it seemed to him that it must have ceased but lately and that it was the sudden cessation which had disturbed him. The fire had fallen low, but still it threw out a deep red glow. As he looked he started in spite of his sangfroid.

There on the great high-backed carved oak chair by the right side of the fireplace sat an enormous rat, steadily glaring at him with baleful eyes. He made a motion to it as though to hunt it away, but it did not stir.

Then he made the motion of throwing something. Still it did not stir, but showed its great white teeth angrily, and its cruel eyes shone in the lamplight with an added vindictiveness.

Malcolmson felt amazed, and seizing the poker from the hearth ran at it to kill it. Before, however, he could strike it, the rat, with a squeak that sounded like the concentration of hate, jumped upon the floor, and, running up the rope of the alarm bell, disappeared in the darkness beyond the range of the green-shaded lamp. Instantly, strange to say, the noisy scampering of the rats in the wainscot began again.

By this time Malcolmson's mind was quite off the problem; and as a shrill cock-crow outside told him of the approach of morning, he went to bed and to sleep.

He slept so soundly that he was not even waked by Mrs. Dempster coming in to make up his room. It was only when she had tidied up the place and got his breakfast ready and tapped on the screen which closed in his bed that he woke. He was a little tired still after his night's hard work, but a strong cup of tea soon freshened him up, and, taking his book, he went out for his morning walk, bringing with him a few sandwiches lest he should not care to return till dinnertime. He found a quiet walk between high elms some way outside the town, and here he spent the greater part of the day studying his Laplace. On his return he looked in to see Mrs. Witham and to thank her for her kindness. When she saw him coming through the diamond-paned bay window of her sanctum she came out to meet him and asked him in. She looked at him searchingly and shook her head as she said:

"You must not overdo it, sir. You are paler this morning than you should be. Too late hours and too hard work on the brain isn't good for any man! But tell me, sir, how did you pass the night? Well, I hope? But, my heart! Sir, I was glad when Mrs. Dempster told me this morning that you were all right and sleeping sound when she went in."

"Oh, I was all right," he answered, smiling, "the 'some-things' didn't worry me, as yet. Only the rats; and they had a circus, I tell you, all over the place. There was one wicked-looking old devil that sat up on my own chair by the fire, and wouldn't go till I took the poker to him, and then he ran up the rope of the alarm bell and got to somewhere up the wall or the ceiling—I couldn't see where, it was so dark."

"Mercy on us," said Mrs. Witham, "an old devil, and sitting on a chair by the fireside! Take care, sir! Take care! There's many a true word spoken in jest."

"How do you mean? 'Pon my word I don't understand."

"An old devil! The old devil, perhaps. There! Sir, you needn't laugh," for Malcolmson had broken into a hearty peal. "You young folks thinks it easy to laugh at things that makes older ones shudder. Never mind, sir! Never mind! Please God, you'll laugh all the time. It's what I wish you myself!" and the good lady beamed all over in sympathy with his enjoyment, her fears gone for a moment.

"Oh, forgive me!" said Malcolmson presently. "Don't think me rude; but the idea was too much for me—that the old devil himself was on the chair last night!" And at the thought he laughed again. Then he went home to dinner.

This evening the scampering of the rats began earlier. Indeed it had been going on before his arrival, and only ceased whilst his presence by its freshness disturbed them. After dinner he sat by the fire for a while and had a smoke; and then, having cleared his table, began to work as before. Tonight the rats disturbed him more than they had done on the previous night. How they scampered up and down and under and over! How they squeaked, and scratched, and gnawed! How they, getting bolder by degrees, came to the mouths of their holes and to the chinks and cracks and crannies in the wainscoting till their eyes shone like tiny lamps as the firelight rose and fell. But to him, now doubtless accustomed to them, their eyes were not wicked; only their playfulness touched him. Sometimes the boldest of them made sallies out on the floor or along the moldings of the wainscot. Now and again as they disturbed him Malcolmson made a sound to frighten them, smiting the table with his hand or giving a fierce "Hsh, hsh," so that they fled straightway to their holes.

And so the early part of the night wore on; and despite the noise Malcolmson got more and more immersed in his work.

All at once he stopped, as on the previous night, being overcome by a sudden sense of silence. There was not the faintest sound of gnaw, or scratch, or squeak. The silence was as of the grave. He remembered the odd occurrence of the previous night, and instinctively he looked at the chair standing close by the fireside. And then a very odd sensation thrilled through him.

There, on the great old high-backed carved oak chair beside the fireplace sat the same enormous rat, steadily glaring at him with baleful eyes.

Instinctively he took the nearest thing to his hand, a

book of logarithms, and flung it at it. The book was badly aimed and the rat did not stir, so again the poker performance of the previous night was repeated; and again the rat, being closely pursued, fled up the rope of the alarm bell. Strangely too, the departure of this rat was instantly followed by the renewal of the noise made by the general rat community. On this occasion, as on the previous one, Malcolmson could not see at what part of the room the rat disappeared, for the green shade of his lamp left the upper part of the room in darkness, and the fire had burned low.

On looking at his watch he found it was close on midnight; and, not sorry for the divertissement, he made up his fire and made himself his nightly pot of tea. He had got through a good spell of work, and thought himself entitled to a cigarette; and so he sat on the great carved oak chair before the fire and enjoyed it. Whilst smoking he began to think that he would like to know where the rat disappeared to, for he had certain ideas for the morrow not entirely disconnected with a rat-trap. Accordingly he lit another lamp and placed it so that it would shine well into the right-hand corner of the wall by the fireplace. Then he got all the books he had with him, and placed them handy to throw at the vermin. Finally he lifted the rope of the alarm bell and placed the end of it on the table, fixing the extreme end under the lamp. As he handled it he could not help noticing how pliable it was, especially for so strong a rope, and one not in use. "You could hang a man with it," he thought to himself. When his preparations were made he looked around, and said complacently:

"There now, my friend, I think we shall learn something of you this time!" He began his work again, and though as before somewhat disturbed at first by the noise of the rats, soon lost himself in his propositions and problems.

Again he was called to his immediate surroundings suddenly. This time it might not have been the sudden silence only which took his attention; there was a slight movement of the rope, and the lamp moved. Without stirring, he looked to see if his pile of books was within range, and then cast his eye along the rope. As he looked he saw the great rat drop from the rope on the oak armchair and sit there glaring at him. He raised a book in his right hand, and taking careful aim, flung it at the rat. The latter, with a quick movement, sprang aside and dodged the missile. He then took another book, and a third, and flung them one after another at the rat, but each time unsuccessfully. At last, as he stood with a book poised in his hand to throw, the rat squeaked and seemed afraid. This made Malcolmson more than ever eager to strike, and the book flew and struck the rat a resounding blow. It gave a terrified squeak, and turning on its pursuer a look of terrible malevolence, ran up the chair-back and made a great jump to the rope of the alarm bell and ran up it like lightning. The lamp rocked under the sudden strain, but it was a heavy one and did not topple over. Malcolmson kept his eyes on the rat, and saw it by the light of the second lamp leap to a molding of the wainscot and disappear through a hole in one of the great pictures which hung on the wall, obscured and invisible through its coating of dirt and dust.

"I shall look up my friend's habitation in the morning," said the student, as he went over to collect his books. "The third picture from the fireplace; I shall not forget." He picked up the books one by one, commenting on them as he lifted them. "Conic Sections he does not mind, nor Cycloidal Oscillations, nor the Principia, nor Quaternions, nor Thermodynamics. Now for the book that fetched him!" Malcolmson took it up and looked at it. As he did so he started, and a sudden pallor overspread his face. He looked round uneasily and shivered slightly, as he murmured to himself:

"The Bible my mother gave me! What an odd coincidence." He sat down to work again, and the rats in the wainscot renewed their gambols. They did not disturb him, however; somehow their presence gave him a sense of companionship. But he could not attend to his work, and after striving to master the subject on which he was engaged gave it up in despair, and went to bed as the first streak of dawn stole in through the eastern window.

He slept heavily but uneasily, and dreamed much; and when Mrs. Dempster woke him late in the morning he seemed ill at ease, and for a few minutes did not seem to realize exactly where he was. His first request rather surprised the servant.

"Mrs. Dempster, when I am out today I wish you would get the steps and dust or wash those pictures— specially that one the third from the fireplace—I want to see what they are." Late in the afternoon Malcolmson worked at his books in the shaded walk, and the cheerfulness of the previous day came back to him as the day wore on, and he found that his reading was progressing well. He had worked out to a satisfactory conclusion all the problems which had as yet baffled him, and it was in a state of jubilation that he paid a visit to Mrs. Witham at "The Good Traveller." He found a stranger in the cozy sitting room with the landlady, who was introduced to him as Dr. Thornhill. She was not quite at ease, and this, combined with the Doctor's plunging at once into a series of questions, made Malcolmson come to the conclusion that his presence was not an accident, so without preliminary he said:

"Dr. Thornhill, I shall with pleasure answer you any question you may choose to ask me if you will answer me one question first."

The Doctor seemed surprised, but he smiled and answered at once. "Done! What is it?"

"Did Mrs. Witham ask you to come here and see me and advise me?"

Dr. Thornhill for a moment was taken aback, and Mrs. Witham got fiery red and turned away; but the Doctor was a frank and ready man, and he answered at once and openly:

"She did: but she didn't intend you to know it. I suppose it was my clumsy haste that made you suspect. She told me that she did not like the idea of your being in that house all by yourself, and that she thought you took too much strong tea. In fact, she wants me to advise you if possible to give up the tea and the very late hours. I was a keen student in my time, so I suppose I may take the liberty of a college man, and without offense, advise you not quite as a stranger."

Malcolmson with a bright smile held out his hand. "Shake! as they say in America," he said. "I must thank you for your kindness and Mrs. Witham too, and your kindness deserves a return on my part. I promise to take no more strong tea—no tea at all till you let me—and I shall go to bed tonight at one o'clock at latest. Will that do?"

"Capital," said the Doctor. "Now tell us all that you noticed in the old house," and so Malcolmson then and there told in minute detail all that had happened in the last two nights. He was interrupted every now and then by some exclamation from Mrs. Witham, till finally when he told of the episode of the Bible the landlady's pent-up emotions found vent in a shriek; and it was not till a stiff glass of brandy and water had been administered that she grew composed again. Dr. Thornhill listened with a face of growing gravity, and when the narrative was complete and Mrs. Witham had been restored he asked:

"The rat always went up the rope of the alarm bell?"

"Always."

"I suppose you know," said the Doctor after a pause, "what the rope is?"

"No!"

"It is," said the Doctor slowly, "the very rope which the hangman used for all the victims of the Judge's judicial rancor!" Here he was interrupted by another scream from Mrs. Witham, and steps had to be taken for her recovery. Malcolmson having looked at his watch, and found that it was close to his dinner hour, had gone home before her complete recovery.

When Mrs. Witham was herself again she almost assailed the Doctor with angry questions as to what he meant by putting such horrible ideas into the poor young man's mind. "He has quite enough there already to upset him," she added. Dr. Thornhill replied:

"My dear madam, I had a distinct purpose in it! I wanted to draw his attention to the bell rope, and to fix it there. It may be that he is in a highly overwrought state, and has been studying too much, although I am bound to say that he seems as sound and healthy a young man,

mentally and bodily, as ever I saw—but then the rats—
and that suggestion of the devil." The Doctor shook his
head and went on. "I would have offered to go and stay
the first night with him but that I felt sure it would have
been a cause of offense. He may get in the night some
strange fright or hallucination; and if he does I want him
to pull that rope. All alone as he is it will give us warning,
and we may reach him in time to be of service. I shall be
sitting up pretty late tonight and shall keep my ears open.
Do not be alarmed if Benchurch gets a surprise before
morning."

"Oh, Doctor, what do you mean? What do you
mean?"

"I mean this; that possibly—nay, more probably—we
shall hear the great alarm bell from the Judge's House
tonight," and the Doctor made about as effective an exit
as could be thought of.

When Malcolmson arrived home he found that it
was a little after his usual time, and Mrs. Dempster had
gone away—the rules of Greenhow's Charity were not to
be neglected. He was glad to see that the place was
bright and tidy with a cheerful fire and a well-trimmed
lamp. The evening was colder than might have been expected in April, and a heavy wind was blowing with such
rapidly increasing strength that there was every promise
of a storm during the night. For a few minutes after his
entrance the noise of the rats ceased; but so soon as they
became accustomed to his presence they began again.
He was glad to hear them, for he felt once more the feeling of companionship in their noise, and his mind ran
back to the strange fact that they only ceased to manifest
themselves when that other—the great rat with the baleful eyes—came upon the scene. The reading lamp only

was lit and its green shade kept the ceiling and the upper part of the room in darkness, so that the cheerful light from the hearth spreading over the floor and shining on the white cloth laid over the end of the table was warm and cheery. Malcolmson sat down to his dinner with a good appetite and a buoyant spirit. After his dinner and a cigarette he sat steadily down to work, determined not to let anything disturb him, for he remembered his promise to the Doctor, and made up his mind to make the best of the time at his disposal.

For an hour or so he worked all right, and then his thoughts began to wander from his books. The actual circumstances around him, the calls on his physical attention, and his nervous susceptibility were not to be denied. By this time the wind had become a gale, and the gale a storm. The old house, solid though it was, seemed to shake to its foundations, and the storm roared and raged through its many chimneys and its queer old gables, producing strange, unearthly sounds in the empty rooms and corridors. Even the great alarm bell on the roof must have felt the force of the wind, for the rope rose and fell slightly, as though the bell were moved a little from time to time, and the limber rope fell on the oak floor with a hard and hollow sound.

As Malcolmson listened to it he bethought himself of the Doctor's words, "It is the rope which the hangman used for the victims of the Judge's judicial rancor," and he went over to the corner of the fireplace and took it in his hand to look at it. There seemed a sort of deadly interest in it, and as he stood there he lost himself for a moment in speculation as to who these victims were, and the grim wish of the Judge to have such a ghastly relic ever under his eyes. As he stood there the swaying of the bell on the roof still lifted the rope now and again; but presently there came a new sensation—a sort of tremor in the rope, as though something was moving along it.

Looking up instinctively Malcolmson saw the great rat coming slowly down toward him, glaring at him steadily. He dropped the rope and started back with a muttered curse, and the rat, turning, ran up the rope again and disappeared, and at the same instant Malcolmson became conscious that the noise of the rats, which had ceased for a while, began again.

All this set him thinking, and it occurred to him that he had not investigated the lair of the rat or looked at the pictures, as he had intended. He lit the other lamp without the shade, and, holding it up, went and stood opposite the third picture from the fireplace on the right-hand side where he had seen the rat disappear on the previous night.

At the first glance he started back so suddenly that he almost dropped the lamp, and a deadly pallor overspread his face. His knees shook, and heavy drops of sweat came on his forehead, and he trembled like an aspen. But he was young and plucky, and pulled himself together, and after the pause of a few seconds stepped forward again, raised the lamp, and examined the picture which had been dusted and washed, and now stood out clearly.

It was of a judge dressed in his robes of scarlet and ermine. His face was strong and merciless, evil, crafty, and vindictive, with a sensual mouth, hooked nose of ruddy color, and shaped like the beak of a bird of prey. The rest of the face was of a cadaverous color. The eyes were of peculiar brilliance and with a terribly malignant expression. As he looked at them, Malcolmson grew cold, for he saw there the very counterpart of the eyes of the great rat. The lamp almost fell from his hand; he saw the rat with its baleful eyes peering out through the hole in the corner of the picture, and noted the sudden cessation of the noise of the other rats. However, he pulled himself together, and went on with his examination of the picture.

The Judge was seated in a great high-backed carved oak chair, on the right-hand side of a great stone fireplace where, in the corner, a rope hung down from the ceiling, its end lying coiled on the floor. With a feeling of something like horror, Malcolmson recognized the scene of the room as it stood, and gazed around him in an awestruck manner as though he expected to find some strange presence behind him. Then he looked over to the corner of the fireplace—and with a loud cry he let the lamp fall from his hand.

There, in the Judge's armchair, with the rope hanging behind, sat the rat with the Judge's baleful eyes, now intensified and with a fiendish leer. Save for the howling of the storm without there was silence.

The fallen lamp recalled Malcolmson to himself. Fortunately it was of metal, and so the oil was not spilled. However, the practical need of attending to it settled at once his nervous apprehensions. When he had turned it out, he wiped his brow and thought for a moment.

"This will not do," he said to himself. "If I go on like this I shall become a crazy fool. This must stop! I promised the Doctor I would not take tea. Faith, he was pretty right! My nerves must have been getting into a queer state. Funny I did not notice it. I never felt better in my life. However, it is all right now, and I shall not be such a fool again."

Then he mixed himself a good stiff glass of brandy
and water and resolutely sat down to his work.

It was nearly an hour when he looked up from his
book, disturbed by the sudden stillness. Without, the wind
howled and roared louder than ever, and the rain drove
in sheets against the windows, beating like hail on the
glass; but within there was no sound whatever save the
echo of the wind as it roared in the great chimney, and
now and then a hiss as a few raindrops found their way
down the chimney in a lull of the storm. The fire had
fallen low and had ceased to flame, though it threw out a
red glow. Malcolmson listened attentively, and presently
heard a thin, squeaking noise, very faint. It came from the
corner of the room where the rope hung down, and he
thought it was the creaking of the rope on the floor as
the swaying of the bell raised and lowered it. Looking up,
however, he saw in the dim light the great rat clinging to
the rope and gnawing it. The rope was already nearly
gnawed through—he could see the lighter color where
the strands were laid bare. As he looked the job was
completed, and the severed end of the rope fell clattering
on the oaken floor, whilst for an instant the great rat remained like a knob or tassel at the end of the rope,
which now began to sway to and fro. Malcolmson felt for
a moment another pang of terror as he thought that now
the possibility of calling the outer world to his assistance
was cut off, but an intense anger took its place, and seizing the book he was reading he hurled it at the rat. The
blow was well aimed, but before the missile could reach
it the rat dropped off and struck the floor with a soft
thud. Malcolmson instantly rushed over toward it, but it
darted away and disappeared in the darkness of the
shadows of the room. Malcolmson felt that his work was

over for the night, and determined then and there to vary the monotony of the proceedings by a hunt for the rat, and took off the green shade of the lamp so as to ensure a wider spreading light. As he did so the gloom of the upper part of the room was relieved, and in the new flood of light, great by comparison with the previous darkness, the pictures on the wall stood out boldly. From where he stood, Malcolmson saw right opposite to him the third picture on the wall from the right of the fireplace. He rubbed his eyes in surprise, and then a great fear began to come upon him.

In the center of the picture was a great irregular patch of brown canvas, as fresh as when it was stretched on the frame. The background was as before, with chair and chimney-corner and rope, but the figure of the Judge had disappeared.

Malcolmson, almost in a chill of horror, turned slowly round, and then he began to shake and tremble like a man in a palsy. His strength seemed to have left him, and he was incapable of action or movement, hardly even of thought. He could only see and hear.

There, on the great high-backed carved oak chair sat the Judge in his robes of scarlet and ermine, with his baleful eyes glaring vindictively, and a smile of triumph on the resolute, cruel mouth, as he lifted with his hands a black cap. Malcolmson felt as if the blood was running from his heart, as one does in moments of prolonged suspense. There was a singing in his ears. Without, he could hear the roar and howl of the tempest, and through it, swept on the storm, came the striking of midnight by the great chimes in the marketplace. He stood for a space of time that seemed to him endless, still as a statue and with wide-open, horror-struck eyes, breathless. As the clock

struck, so the smile of triumph on the Judge's face intensified, and at the last stroke of midnight he placed the
black cap on his head.

Slowly and deliberately the Judge rose from his chair
and picked up the piece of the rope of the alarm bell
which lay on the floor, drew it through his hands as if he
enjoyed its touch, and then deliberately began to knot
one end of it, fashioning it into a noose. This he tightened and tested with his foot, pulling hard at it till he was
satisfied and then making a running noose of it, which he
held in his hand. Then he began to move along the table
on the opposite side to Malcolmson, keeping his eyes on
him until he had passed him, when with a quick movement he stood in front of the door. Malcolmson then began to feel that he was trapped, and tried to think of what
he should do. There was some fascination in the Judge's
eyes, which he never took off him, and he had, perforce,
to look. He saw the Judge approach—still keeping between him and the door—and raise the noose and throw
it toward him as if to entangle him. With a great effort he
made a quick movement to one side, and saw the rope
fall beside him, and heard it strike the oaken floor. Again
the Judge raised the noose and tried to ensnare him, ever
keeping his baleful eyes fixed on him, and each time by a
mighty effort the student just managed to evade it. So this
went on for many times, the Judge seeming never dis-
couraged nor discomposed at failure, but playing as a cat
does with a mouse. At last in despair, which had reached
its climax, Malcolmson cast a quick glance round him.
The lamp seemed to have blazed up, and there was a
fairly good light in the room. At the many rat-holes and in
the chinks and crannies of the wainscot he saw the rats'
eyes; and this aspect, that was purely physical, gave him

a gleam of comfort. He looked around and saw that the rope of the great alarm bell was laden with rats. Every inch of it was covered with them, and more and more were pouring through the small circular hole in the ceiling whence it emerged, so that with their weight the bell was beginning to sway.

Hark! It had swayed till the clapper had touched the bell. The sound was but a tiny one, but the bell was only beginning to sway, and it would increase.

At the sound the Judge, who had been keeping his eyes fixed on Malcolmson, looked up, and a scowl of diabolical anger overspread his face. His eyes fairly glowed like hot coals, and he stamped his foot with a sound that seemed to make the house shake. A dreadful peal of thunder broke overhead as he raised the rope again, while the rats kept running up and down the rope as though working against time. This time, instead of throwing it, he drew close to his victim, and held open the noose as he approached. As he came closer there seemed something paralyzing in his very presence, and Malcolmson stood rigid as a corpse. He felt the Judge's icy fingers touch his throat as he adjusted the rope. The noose tightened—tightened. Then the Judge, taking the rigid form of the student in his arms, carried him over and placed him standing in the oak chair, and stepping up beside him, put his hand up and caught the end of the swaying rope of the alarm bell. As he raised his hand the rats fled squeaking, and disappeared through the hole in the ceiling. Taking the end of the noose which was round Malcolmson's neck he tied it to the hanging bell rope, and then descending pulled away the chair.

*　*　*

When the alarm bell of the Judge's House began to sound a crowd soon assembled. Lights and torches of various kinds appeared, and soon a silent crowd was hurrying to the spot. They knocked loudly at the door, but there was no reply. Then they burst in the door, and poured into the great dining room, the Doctor at the head.

There at the end of the rope of the great alarm bell hung the body of the student, and on the face of the Judge in the picture was a malignant smile.

The Tell-Tale Heart

Edgar Allan Poe
(1809–1849)

A precarious beginning. An impoverished middle. A ghastly end. Edgar Allan Poe's life story reads like he penned it himself. At the time of his birth, his father ran away, and three years later, his mother died of tuberculosis. Taken in and cared for by John Allan and family, he eventually disgraced them with antisocial behavior at the University of Virginia. He later moved to New York where he lived in poverty as he wrote insatiably and while his cousin-bride wasted away. He gave away such masterpieces as "The Raven" or sold them for scant amounts. His literary career as a whole was anything but successful in monetary terms, but his style in detail and character development were most masterful, delicate, and precise. He was a capable editor. He was also prolific, writing a science fiction novel and more than a hundred short stories and poems in only twenty years. What was he not? By many accounts, he was not capable of handling the details of daily life. At the age of forty, he disappeared and was found dying in a Baltimore gutter. A dreadful, lonely end for a literary master. The tales and rumors about Poe's life filled the streets soon after his death, but his work has left an everlasting legacy. "The Tell-Tale Heart" is a beloved American classic. No macabre collection, big or small, would be complete without it.

*T*rue—nervous— very, very dreadfully nervous I had been and am! But why *will* you say that I am mad? The disease had sharpened my senses, not destroyed, not dulled them. Above all was the sense of hearing acute. I heard all things in the heaven and in the earth. I heard many things in hell. How, then, am I mad? Hearken and observe how healthily—how calmly—I can tell you the whole story.

It is impossible to say how first the idea entered my brain; but once conceived, it haunted me day and night. Object there was none. Passion there was none. I loved the old man. He had never wronged me. He had never given me insult. For his gold I had no desire. I think it was his eye! Yes, it was this! One of his eyes resembled that of a vulture—a pale blue eye, with a film over it. Whenever it fell upon me, my blood ran cold; and so by degrees—very gradually—I made up my mind to take the life of the old man, and thus rid myself of the eye forever.

Now this is the point. You fancy me mad. Madmen know nothing. But you should have seen *me*. You should have seen how wisely I proceeded, with what caution, with what foresight, with what dissimulation I went to work!

I was never kinder to the old man during the whole

week before I killed him. And every night, about mid-night, I turned the latch of his door and opened it—oh, so gently! And then, when I had made an opening suffi-cient for my head, I put in a dark lantern, all closed, closed, so that no light shone out, and then I thrust in my head. Oh, you would have laughed to see how cunningly I thrust it in! I moved it slowly—very slowly, so that I might not disturb the old man's sleep. It took me an hour to place my whole head within the opening so far that I could see him as he lay upon his bed. Ha! Would a mad-man have been so wise as this? And then, when my head was well in the room, I undid the lantern cautiously—oh, so cautiously—cautiously (for the hinges creaked)—I un-did it just so much that a single thin ray fell upon the vul-ture eye. And this I did for seven long nights—every night just at midnight—but I found the eye always closed; and so it was impossible to do the work; for it was not the old man who vexed me, but his Evil Eye. And every morning, when the day broke, I went boldly into the chamber, and spoke courageously to him, calling him by name in a hearty tone, and inquiring how he had passed the night. So you see he would have been a very pro-found old man, indeed, to suspect that every night, just at twelve, I looked in upon him while he slept.

Upon the eighth night I was more than usually cau-tious in opening the door. A watch's minute hand moves more quickly than did mine. Never before that night had I *felt* the extent of my own powers, of my sagacity. I could scarcely contain my feelings of triumph. To think that there I was, opening the door, little by little, and he not even to dream of my secret deeds or thoughts. I fairly chuckled at the idea; and perhaps he heard me; for he moved on the bed suddenly, as if startled. Now you may

think that I drew back—but no. His room was as black as
pitch with the thick darkness (for the shutters were close
fastened, through fear of robbers) and so I knew that he
could not see the opening of the door, and I kept pushing it on steadily, steadily.

I had my head in, and was about to open the lantern,
when my thumb slipped upon the tin fastening, and the
old man sprang up in bed, crying out: "Who's there?"

I kept quite still and said nothing. For a whole hour I
did not move a muscle, and in the meantime I did not hear
him lie down. He was still sitting up in the bed listening—
just as I have done, night after night, hearkening to the
death watches in the wall.

Presently I heard a slight groan, and I knew it was the
groan of mortal terror. It was not a groan of pain or of
grief—oh no!—it was the low stifled sound that arises
from the bottom of the soul when overcharged with awe.
I knew the sound well. Many a night, just at midnight,
when all the world slept, it has welled up from my own
bosom, deepening, with its dreadful echo, the terrors that
distracted me. I say I knew it well. I knew what the old
man felt, and pitied him, although I chuckled at heart. I
knew that he had been lying awake ever since the first
slight noise, when he had turned in the bed. His fears
had been ever since growing upon him. He had been
trying to fancy them causeless, but could not. He had
been saying to himself, "It is nothing but the wind in the
chimney—it is only a mouse crossing the floor," or, "It is
merely a cricket which has made a single chirp." Yes, he
had been trying to comfort himself with these supposi-
tions; but he had found all in vain. *All in vain;* because
Death, in approaching him, had stalked with his black
shadow before him, and enveloped the victim. And it

was the mournful influence of the unperceived shadow that caused him to feel—although he neither saw nor heard—to *feel* the presence of my head within the room.

When I had waited a long time, very patiently, without hearing him lie down, I resolved to open a little—a very, very little—crevice in the lantern. So I opened it— you cannot imagine how stealthily, stealthily—until, at length, a single dim ray, like the thread of the spider, shot from out the crevice and full upon the vulture eye.

It was open—wide, wide open—and I grew furious as I gazed upon it. I saw it with perfect distinctness, all a dull blue, with a hideous evil veil over it that chilled the very marrow in my bones, but I could see nothing else of the old man's face or person: for I had directed the ray as if by instinct, precisely upon the damned spot.

And now have I not told you that what you mistake for madness is but over-acuteness of the senses? Now, I say, there came to my ears a low, dull, quick sound, such as a watch makes when enveloped in cotton. I knew *that* sound well too. It was the beating of the old man's heart. It increased my fury, as the beating of a drum stimulates the soldier into courage.

But even yet I refrained and kept still. I scarcely breathed. I held the lantern motionless. I tried how steadily I could maintain the ray upon the eye. Meantime the hellish tattoo of the heart increased. It grew quicker and quicker, and louder and louder every instant. The old man's terror *must* have been extreme! It grew louder, I say, louder every moment! Do you mark me well? I have told you that I am nervous: so I am. And now at the dead hour of the night, amid the dreadful silence of that old house, so strange a noise as this excited me to uncontrollable terror. Yet, for some minutes longer I refrained and stood still. But the beating grew louder, louder! I thought the heart must burst. And now a new anxiety seized me—the sound would be heard by a neighbor! The old man's hour had come! With a loud yell, I threw open the lantern and leaped into the room. He shrieked once, once only. In an instant I dragged him to the floor, and pulled the heavy bed over him. I then smiled gaily, to find the deed so far done. But, for many minutes, the heart beat on with a muffled sound. This, however, did not vex me; it would not be heard through the wall. At length it ceased. The old man was dead. I removed the bed and examined the corpse. Yes, he was stone, stone dead. I placed my hand upon the heart and held it there many minutes. There was no pulsation. He was stone dead. His eye would trouble me no more.

If still you think me mad, you will think so no longer when I describe the wise precautions I took for the concealment of the body. The night waned, and I worked hastily, but in silence. First of all I dismembered the corpse. I cut off the head and the arms and the legs.

I then took up three planks from the flooring of the chamber, and deposited all between the scantlings. I then replaced the boards so cleverly, so cunningly, that no human eye—not even *his*—could have detected anything wrong. There was nothing to wash out—no stain of any kind—no blood-spot whatever. I had been too wary for that. A tub had caught all—ha! ha!

When I had made an end of these labors, it was four o'clock—still dark as midnight. As the bell sounded the hour, there came a knocking at the street door. I went down to open it with a light heart, for what had I *now* to fear? There entered three men, who introduced themselves, with perfect suavity, as officers of the police. A shriek had been heard by a neighbor during the night; suspicion of foul play had been aroused; information had been lodged at the police station and they (the officers) had been deputed to search the premises.

I smiled, for *what* had I to fear? I bade the gentlemen welcome. The shriek, I said, was my own in a dream. The old man, I mentioned, was absent in the country. I took my visitors all over the house. I bade them search— search *well.* I led them, at length, to *his* chamber. I showed them his treasures, secure, undisturbed. In the enthusiasm of my confidence, I brought chairs into the room, and desired them *here* to rest from their fatigue, while I myself, in the wild audacity of my perfect triumph, placed my own seat upon the very spot beneath which reposed the corpse of the victim.

The officers were satisfied. My *manner* had convinced them. I was singularly at ease. They sat, and while I answered cheerily, they chatted about familiar things. But, ere long, I felt myself getting pale and wished them gone. My head ached, and I fancied a ringing in my ears: but still they sat and still they chatted. The ringing became more distinct: it continued and became more distinct. I talked more freely to get rid of the feeling: but it continued and gained definitiveness—until at length, I found that the noise was *not* within my ears.

No doubt I now grew *very* pale—but I talked more fluently, and with a heightened voice. Yet the sound increased, and what could I do? It was *a low, dull, quick sound—much such a sound as a watch makes when enveloped in cotton.* I gasped for breath, and yet the officers heard it not. I talked more quickly—more vehemently; but the noise steadily increased. I arose and argued about trifles, in a high key and with violent gesticulations, but the noise steadily increased. Why *would* they not be gone? I paced the floor to and fro with heavy strides, as if excited to fury by the observation of the men—but the noise steadily increased. Oh God! What *could* I do? I foamed—I raved—I swore! I swung the chair upon which I had been sitting, and grated it upon the boards, but the noise arose over all and continually increased. It grew louder—louder—*louder!* And still the men chatted pleasantly, and smiled. Was it possible they heard not? Almighty God, no, no! They heard! They suspected! They *knew!* They were making a *mockery* of my horror! This I thought, and this I think. But anything was better than this agony! Anything was more tolerable than this derision! I could bear those hypocritical smiles no longer! I felt that I must scream or die, and now—again—hark! Louder, louder, louder, *louder!*

"Villains," I shrieked, "dissemble no more! I admit the deed! Tear up the planks! Here, here! It is the beating of his hideous heart!"

The Cold Embrace

Mary Elizabeth Braddon
(1835–1915)

The mother of six, the stepmother of five, Mary Elizabeth Braddon
was a remarkably prolific writer of the Victorian era. She gave up
a stage career to become a full-time writer in her efforts to support
her mother. Between 1861 and 1871, she wrote twenty novels,
and by the 1880s her publisher boasted that she had forty-three
novels in print. *Lady Audley's Secret*, along with several other
Braddon novels, still graces bookstore shelves, and her short stories
and stories of the supernatural are readily anthologized. I selected
"The Cold Embrace," a short, poignant story of how the
ghosts of deceit can hang about one's neck.

*H*e was an artist—such things as happened to him happen sometimes to artists.

He was a German—such things as happened to him happen sometimes to Germans.

He was young, handsome, studious, enthusiastic, metaphysical, reckless, unbelieving, heartless.

And being young, handsome, and eloquent, he was beloved.

He was an orphan, under the guardianship of his dead father's brother, his uncle Wilhelm, in whose house he had been brought up from a little child; and she who loved him was his cousin—his cousin Gertrude, whom he swore he loved in return.

Did he love her? Yes, when he first swore it. It soon wore out, this passionate love; how threadbare and wretched a sentiment it became at last in the selfish heart of the student! But in its golden dawn, when he was only nineteen, and had just returned from his apprenticeship to a great painter at Antwerp, and they wandered together in the most romantic outskirts of the city at rosy sunset, by holy moonlight, or bright and joyous morning, how beautiful a dream!

They keep it a secret from Wilhelm, as he has the father's ambition of a wealthy suitor for his only child—a cold and dreary vision beside the lover's dream.

So they are betrothed; and standing side by side when the dying sun and the pale rising moon divide the heavens, he puts the betrothal ring upon her finger, the white and tapered finger whose slender shape he knows so well. This ring is a peculiar one, a massive golden serpent, its tail in its mouth, the symbol of eternity; it had been his mother's, and he would know it amongst a thousand. If he were to become blind tomorrow, he could select it from amongst a thousand by the touch alone.

He places it on her finger, and they swear to be true to each other forever and ever—through trouble and danger—sorrow and change—in wealth or poverty. Her father must needs be won to consent to their union by and by, for they were now betrothed, and death alone could part them.

But the young student, the scoffer at revelation, yet the enthusiastic adorer of the mystical, asks:

"Can death part us? I would return to you from the grave, Gertrude. My soul would come back to be near my love. And you—you, if you died before me—the cold earth would not hold you from me. If you loved me, you would return, and again these fair arms would be clasped round my neck as they are now."

But she told him, with a holier light in her deep-blue eyes than had ever shone in his—she told him that the dead who die at peace with God are happy in heaven, and cannot return to the troubled earth; and that it is only the suicide—the lost wretch on whom sorrowful angels shut the door of Paradise—whose unholy spirit haunts the footsteps of the living.

*   *   *

The first year of their betrothal is passed, and she is alone, for he has gone to Italy, on a commission for some rich man, to copy Raphaels, Titians, Guidos, in a gallery at Florence. He has gone to win fame, perhaps; but it is not the less bitter—he is gone!

Of course her father misses his young nephew, who has been as a son to him; and he thinks his daughter's sadness no more than a cousin should feel for a cousin's absence.

In the meantime, the weeks and months pass. The lover writes—often at first, then seldom—at last, not at all.

How many excuses she invents for him! How many times she goes to the distant little post office, to which he is to address his letters! How many times she hopes, only to be disappointed! How many times she despairs, only to hope again!

But real despair comes at last, and will not be put off anymore. The rich suitor appears on the scene, and her father is determined. She is to marry at once. The wedding-day is fixed—the fifteenth of June.

The date seems to burn into her brain.

The date, written in fire, dances forever before her eyes.

The date, shrieked by the Furies, sounds continually in her ears.

But there is time yet—it is the middle of May—there is time for a letter to reach him at Florence; there is time for him to come to Brunswick, to take her away and marry her, in spite of her father—in spite of the whole world.

But the days and the weeks fly by, and he does not write—he does not come. This is indeed despair which usurps her heart, and will not be put away.

It is the fourteenth of June. For the last time she goes to the little post office; for the last time she asks the old question, and they give her for the last time the dreary answer, "No, no letter."

For the last time—for tomorrow is the day appointed for the bridal. Her father will hear no entreaties; her rich suitor will not listen to her prayers. They will not be put off a day—an hour; tonight alone is hers—this night, which she may employ as she will.

She takes another path than that which leads home; she hurries through some by-streets of the city, out onto a lonely bridge, where he and she had stood so often in the sunset, watching the rose-colored light glow, fade, and die upon the river.

He returns from Florence. He had received her letter. That letter, blotted with tears, entreating, despairing—he had received it, but he loved her no longer. A young Florentine, who has sat to him for a model, had bewitched his fancy—that fancy which with him stood in place of a heart—and Gertrude had been half-forgotten. If she had a rich suitor, good; let her marry him; better for her, better far for himself. He had no wish to fetter himself with a wife. Had he not his art always?—his eternal bride, his unchanging mistress.

Thus he thought it wiser to delay his journey to Brunswick, so that he should arrive when the wedding was over—arrive in time to salute the bride.

And the vows—the mystical fancies—the belief in his return, even after death, to the embrace of his beloved? O, gone out of his life; melted away forever, those foolish dreams of his boyhood.

So on the fifteenth of June he enters Brunswick, by

that very bridge on which she stood, the stars looking down on her, the night before. He strolls across the bridge and down by the water's edge, a great rough dog at his heels, and the smoke from his short meerschaum-pipe curling in blue wreaths fantastically in the pure morning air. He has his sketchbook under his arm, and attracted now and then by some object that catches his artist's eye, stops to draw: a few weeds and pebbles on the river's brink—a crag on the opposite shore—a group of pollard willows in the distance. When he has done, he admires his drawing, shuts his sketchbook, empties the ashes from his pipe, refills from his tobacco pouch, sings the refrain of a gay drinking-song, calls to his dog, smokes again, and walks on. Suddenly he opens his sketchbook again. This time that which attracts him is a group of figures: but what is it?

It is not a funeral, for there are no mourners.

It is not a funeral, but a corpse lying on a rude bier, covered with an old sail, carried between two bearers.

It is not a funeral, for the bearers are fishermen—fishermen in their everyday garb.

About a hundred yards from him they rest their burden on a bank—one stands at the head of the bier, the other throws himself down at the foot of it.

And thus they form the perfect group. He walks back two or three paces, selects his point of sight, and begins to sketch a hurried outline. He has finished it before they move; he hears their voices, though he cannot hear their words, and wonders what they can be talking of. Presently he walks on and joins them.

"You have a corpse there, my friends?" he says.

"Yes; a corpse washed ashore an hour ago."

"Drowned?"

"Yes, drowned. A young girl, very handsome."

"Suicides are always handsome," says the painter; and then he stands for a little while idly smoking and meditating, looking at the sharp outline of the corpse and the stiff folds of the rough canvas covering.

Life is such a golden holiday for him—young, ambitious, clever—that it seems as though sorrow and death could have no part in his destiny.

At last he says that, as this poor suicide is so handsome, he should like to make a sketch of her.

He gives the fishermen some money, and they offer to remove the sailcloth that covers her features.

No; he will do it himself. He lifts the rough, coarse, wet canvas from her face. What face?

The face that shone on the dreams of his foolish boyhood; the face which once was the light of his uncle's home. His cousin Gertrude—his betrothed!

He sees, as in one glance, while he draws one breath, the rigid features—the marble arms—the hands crossed on the cold bosom; and, on the third finger of the left hand, the ring which had been his mother's—the golden serpent; the ring which, if he were to become blind, he could select from a thousand others by the touch alone.

But he is a genius and a metaphysician—grief, true grief, is not for such as he. His first thought is flight—flight anywhere out of that accursed city—anywhere far from the brink of that hideous river—anywhere away from remorse—anywhere to forget.

He is miles on the road that leads away from Brunswick before he knows that he has walked a step.

It is only when his dog lies down panting at his feet that he feels how exhausted he is himself, and sits down

upon a bank to rest. How the landscape spins round
and round before his dazzled eyes, while his morning's
sketch of the two fishermen and the canvas-covered bier
glares redly at him out of the twilight.

At last, after sitting a long time by the roadside, idly
playing with his dog, idly smoking, idly lounging, looking
as any idle, light-hearted traveling student might look, yet
all the while acting over that morning's scene in his burning brain a hundred times a minute; at last he grows a little more composed, and tries presently to think of himself
as he is, apart from his cousin's suicide. Apart from that,
he was no worse off than he was yesterday. His genius
was not gone; the money he had earned at Florence still
lined his pocketbook; he was his own master, free to go
whither he would.

And while he sits on the roadside, trying to separate
himself from the scene of that morning—trying to put
away the image of the corpse covered with the damp
canvas sail—trying to think of what he should do next,
where he should go, to be farthest away from Brunswick
and remorse, the old diligence comes rumbling and jin-
gling along. He remembers it; it goes from Brunswick to
Aix-la-Chapelle.

He whistles to the dog, shouts to the postillion to
stop, and springs into the coupé.

During the whole evening, through the long night,
though he does not once close his eyes, he never speaks
a word; but when morning dawns, and the other passen-
gers awake and begin to talk to each other, he joins in
the conversation. He tells them that he is an artist, that he
is going to Cologne and to Antwerp to copy Rubenses,
and the great picture by Quentin Matsys, in the museum.
He remembered afterwards that he talked and laughed

boisterously, and that when he was talking and laughing loudest, a passenger, older and graver than the rest, opened the window near him, and told him to put his head out. He remembered the fresh air blowing in his face, the singing of the birds in his ears, and the flat fields and roadside reeling before his eyes. He remembered this, and then falling in a lifeless heap on the floor of the diligence.

It is a fever that keeps him for six long weeks on a bed at a hotel in Aix-la-Chapelle.

He gets well, and, accompanied by his dog, starts on foot for Cologne. By this time he is his former self once more. Again the blue smoke from his short meerschaum curls upwards in the morning air—again he sings some old university drinking song—again stops here and there, meditating and sketching.

He is happy, and has forgotten his cousin—and so on to Cologne.

It is by the great cathedral he is standing, with his dog at his side. It is night, the bells have just chimed the hour, and the clocks are striking eleven; the moonlight shines full upon the magnificent pile, over which the artist's eye wanders, absorbed in the beauty of form.

He is not thinking of his drowned cousin, for he has forgotten her and is happy.

Suddenly someone, something from behind him, puts two cold arms round his neck, and clasps its hands on his breast.

And yet there is no one behind him, for on the flags bathed in the broad moonlight there are only two shadows, his own and his dog's. He turns quickly round—there is no one—nothing to be seen in the broad square but himself and his dog; and though he feels, he cannot see the cold arms clasped round his neck.

It is not ghostly, this embrace, for it is palpable to the touch—it cannot be real, for it is invisible.

He tries to throw off the cold caress. He clasps the hands in his own to tear them asunder, and to cast them off his neck. He can feel the long delicate fingers cold and wet beneath his touch, and on the third finger of the left hand he can feel the ring which was his mother's—the golden serpent—the ring which he has always said he would know among a thousand by the touch alone. He knows it now!

His dead cousin's cold arms are round his neck—his dead cousin's wet hands are clasped upon his breast. He asks himself if he is mad. "Up, Leo!" he shouts. "Up, up, boy!" and the Newfoundland leaps to his shoulders—the dog's paws are on the dead hands, and the animal utters a terrific howl, and springs away from his master.

The student stands in the moonlight, the dead arms around his neck, and the dog at a little distance moaning piteously.

Presently a watchman, alarmed by the howling of the dog, comes into the square to see what is wrong.

In a breath the cold arms are gone.

He takes the watchman home to the hotel with him and gives him money; in his gratitude he could have given the man half his little fortune.

Will it ever come to him again, this embrace of the dead?

He tries never to be alone; he makes a hundred acquaintances, and shares the chamber of another student. He starts up if he is left by himself in the public room of the inn where he is staying, and runs into the street. People notice his strange actions, and begin to think that he is mad.

But, in spite of all, he is alone once more; for one night the public room being empty for a moment, when on some idle pretense he strolls into the street, the street is empty too, and for the second time he feels the cold arms round his neck, and for the second time, when he calls his dog, the animal shrinks away from him with a piteous howl.

After this he leaves Cologne, still traveling on foot—of necessity now, for his money is getting low. He joins traveling hawkers, he walks side by side with laborers, he talks to every foot-passenger he falls in with, and tries from morning till night to get company on the road.

At night he sleeps by the fire in the kitchen of the inn at which he stops; but do what he will, he is often alone, and it is now a common thing for him to feel the cold arms around his neck.

Many months have passed since his cousin's death—autumn, winter, early spring. His money is nearly gone, his health is utterly broken, he is the shadow of his former self, and he is getting near to Paris. He will reach that city at the time of the Carnival. To this he looks forward. In Paris, in Carnival time, he need never, surely, be alone, never feel that deadly caress; he may even recover his lost gaiety, his lost health, once more resume his profession, once more earn fame and money by his art.

How hard he tries to get over the distance that divides him from Paris, while day by day he grows weaker, and his step slower and more heavy!

But there is an end at last. The long dreary roads are passed. This is Paris, which he enters for the first time—Paris, of which he has dreamed so much—Paris, whose million voices are to exorcise his phantom.

To him tonight Paris seems one vast chaos of lights,

music, and confusion—lights which dance before his eyes and will not be still—music that rings in his ears and deafens him—confusion which makes his head whirl round and round.

But, in spite of all, he finds the opera house, where there is a masked ball. He has enough money left to buy a ticket of admission, and to hire a domino to throw over his shabby dress. It seems only a moment after his entering the gates of Paris that he is in the very midst of all the wild gaiety of the opera house ball.

No more darkness, no more loneliness, but a mad crowd, shouting and dancing, and a lovely Débardeuse hanging on his arm.

The boisterous gaiety he feels surely is his old lightheartedness come back. He hears the people around him talking of the outrageous conduct of some drunken student, and it is to him they point when they say this— to him, who has not moistened his lips since yesterday at noon, for even now he will not drink; though his lips are parched, and his throat burning, he cannot drink. His voice is thick and hoarse, and his utterance indistinct; but still this must be his old light-heartedness come back that makes him so wildly gay.

The little Débardeuse is wearied out—her arm rests on his shoulder heavier than lead—the other dancers one by one drop off.

The lights in the chandeliers one by one die out.

The decorations look pale and shadowy in that dim light which is neither night nor day.

A faint glimmer from the dying lamps, a pale streak of cold grey light from the newborn day, creeping in through half-opened shutters.

And by this light the bright-eyed Débardeuse fades

sadly. He looks her in the face. How the brightness of her eyes dies out! Again he looks her in the face. How white that face has grown! Again—and now it is the shadow of a face alone that looks in his.

Again—and they are gone—the bright eyes, the face, the shadow of the face. He is alone; alone in that vast saloon.

Alone, and, in the terrible silence, he hears the echoes of his own footsteps in that dismal dance which has no music.

No music but the beating of his breast. The cold arms are round his neck—they whirl him round, they will not be flung off, or cast away; he can no more escape from their icy grasp than he can escape from death. He looks behind him—there is nothing but himself in the great empty salle; but he can feel—cold, deathlike, but O, how palpable!—the long slender fingers, and the ring which was his mother's.

He tries to shout, but he has no power in his burning throat. The silence of the place is only broken by the echoes of his own footsteps in the dance from which he cannot extricate himself. Who says he has no partner? The cold hands are clasped on his breast, and now he does not shun their caress. No! One more polka, if he drops down dead.

The lights are all out, and, half an hour after, the gendarmes come in with a lantern to see that the house is empty. They are followed by a great dog that they have found seated howling on the steps of the theater. Near the principal entrance they stumble over—

The body of a student, who has died from want of food, exhaustion, and the breaking of a blood vessel.

The Cedar Closet

Lafcadio Hearn
(1850–1904)

Lafcadio Hearn was born on the Greek island of Lefkas to an Anglo-Irish surgeon major in the British army and a Greek mother. At nineteen, he moved to Cincinnati, Ohio, where he eventually became a newspaper reporter. During his twenties, he also edited the *Ye Giglampzia,* a weekly illustrated journal devoted to art, literature, and satire. It was during this time when he became competent in translating literature, and in 1890 Harper Publishing sent him to Japan, where he embraced the culture and renounced the materialism of the West. His writings became the West's greatest intellectual portal to this newly opened country. Hearn became a Japanese citizen, married a Japanese woman, and took the name Yakumo Koizumi. He was, and still is, considered a national treasure by the Japanese. Hearn found tranquillity and spirituality in his new land; he was never noted for writing horror stories. Still . . . "The Cedar Closet" was penned at the beginning of his career, in 1874, when he was a young editor and reporter in Ohio. Within the cedar walls is the bizarre secret of how a mother, by a twisted logic, preserves her husband and child.

It happened ten years ago, and it stands out, and ever will stand out, in my memory like some dark, awful barrier dividing the happy, gleeful years of girlhood, with their foolish, petulant sorrows and eager, innocent joys, and the bright, lovely life which has been mine since. In looking back, that time seems to me shadowed by a dark and terrible brooding cloud, bearing in its lurid gloom what, but for love and patience the tenderest and most untiring, might have been the bolt of death, or, worse a thousand times, of madness. As it was, for months after "life crept on a broken wing," if not "through cells of madness," yet verily "through haunts of horror and fear." O, the weary, weary days and months when I longed piteously for rest! When sunshine was torture, and every shadow filled with horror unspeakable; when my soul's craving was for death; to be allowed to creep away from the terror which lurked in the softest murmur of the summer breeze, the flicker of the shadow of the tiniest leaf on the sunny grass, in every corner and curtain-fold in my dear old home. But love conquered all, and I can tell my story now, with awe and wonder, it is true, but quietly and calmly.

Ten years ago I was living with my only brother in one of the quaint, ivy-grown, red-gabled rectories which are so picturesquely scattered over the fair breadth of England. We were orphans, Archibald and I; and I had been the busy, happy mistress of his pretty home for only one year after leaving school, when Robert Draye asked me to be his wife. Robert and Archie were old friends, and my new home, Draye Court, was only separated from the parsonage by an old gray wall, a low iron-studded door in which admitted us from the sunny parsonage dawn to the old, old park which had belonged to the Drayes for centuries. Robert was lord of the manor; and it was he who had given Archie the living of Draye in the Wold.

It was the night before my wedding day, and our pretty home was crowded with the wedding guests. We were all gathered in the large old-fashioned drawing room after dinner. When Robert left us late in the evening, I walked with him, as usual, to the little gate for what he called our last parting; we lingered awhile under the great walnut tree, through the heavy, somber branches of which the September moon poured its soft pure light. With his last good-night kiss on my lips and my heart full of him and the love which warmed and glorified the whole world for me, I did not care to go back to share in the fun and frolic in the drawing room, but went softly upstairs to my own room. I say "my own room," but I was to occupy it as a bedroom tonight for the first time. It was a pleasant south room, wainscoted in richly carved cedar, which gave the atmosphere a spicy fragrance. I had chosen it as my morning room on my arrival in our home; here I had read and sang and painted, and spent long, sunny hours while Archibald was busy in his study after breakfast. I had had a bed arranged there as I preferred being alone to sharing my own larger bedroom with two of my bridesmaids. It looked bright and cozy as I came in; my favorite low chair was drawn before the fire, whose rosy light glanced and flickered on the glossy dark walls, which gave the room its name, "The Cedar Closet." My maid was busy preparing my toilet table; I sent her away, and sat down to wait for my brother, who I knew would come to bid me good night. He came; we had our last fireside talk in my girlhood's home; and when he left me there was an incursion of all my bridesmaids for a "dressing-gown reception."

When at last I was alone I drew back the curtain and curled myself up on the low wide window seat. The moon was at its brightest. The little church and quiet churchyard beyond the lawn looked fair and calm beneath its rays. The gleam of the white headstones here and there between the trees might have reminded me that life is not all peace and joy—that tears and pain, fear, and parting, have their share in its story—but it did not. The tranquil happiness with which my heart was full overflowed in some soft tears which had no tinge of bitterness, and when at last I did lie down, peace, deep and perfect, still seemed to flow in on me with the moonbeams which filled the room, shimmering on the folds of my bridal dress, which was laid ready for the morning. I am thus minute in describing my last waking moments, that it may be understood that what followed was not creation of a morbid fancy.

I do not know how long I had been asleep, when I was suddenly, as it were, wrenched back to consciousness. The moon had set, the room was quite dark. I could just distinguish the glimmer of a clouded, starless sky through the open window. I could not see or hear anything unusual, but not the less was I conscious of an unwonted, a baleful presence near; an indescribable horror

cramped the very beatings of my heart. With every instant
the certainty grew that my room was shared by some evil
being. I could not cry for help, though Archie's room
was so close, and I knew that one call through the deathlike stillness would bring him to me. All I could do was
to gaze, gaze, gaze into the darkness. Suddenly—and a
throb stung through every nerve—I heard distinctly from
behind the wainscot against which the head of my bed
was placed a low, hollow moan, followed on the instant
by a cackling, malignant laugh from the other side of the
room. If I had been one of the monumental figures in the
little churchyard on which I had seen the quiet moonbeams shine a few hours before I could not have been
more utterly unable to move or speak. Every other faculty
seemed to be lost in the one intent strain of eye and ear.
There came at last the sound of a halting step, the tapping of a crutch upon the floor, then stillness, and slowly,
gradually the room filled with light—a pale, cold, steady
light. Everything around was exactly as I had last seen it
in the mingled shine of the moon and fire, and though I
heard at intervals the harsh laugh, the curtain at the foot
of the bed hid from me whatever uttered it. Again, low
but distinct, the piteous moan broke forth, followed by
some words in a foreign tongue, and with the sound a
figure started from behind the curtain—a dwarfed, deformed woman, dressed in a loose robe of black, sprin-
kled with golden stars, which gave forth a dull, fiery
gleam, in the mysterious light; one lean, yellow hand
clutched the curtain of my bed. It glittered with jeweled
rings—long black hair fell in heavy masses from a golden
circlet over the stunted form. I saw it all clearly as I now
see the pen which writes these words and the hand
which guides it. The face was turned from me, bent

aside, as if greedily drinking in those astonished moans. I noted even the streaks of gray in the long tresses, as I lay helpless in dumb, bewildered horror.

"Again!" she said hoarsely, as the sounds died away into indistinct murmurs, and advancing a step she tapped sharply with a crutch on the cedar wainscot; then again louder and more purposeful rose the wild beseeching voice; this time the words were English.

"Mercy, have mercy! Not on me, but on my child, my little one; she never harmed you. She is dying—she is dying here in darkness; let me but see her face once more. Death is very near, nothing can save her now; but grant one ray of light, and I will pray that you may be forgiven, if forgiveness there be for such as you.

"What, you kneel at last! Kneel to Gerda, and kneel in vain. A ray of light; not if you could pay for it in diamonds. You are mine! Shriek and call as you will, no other ears can hear. Die together. You are mine to torture as I will; mine, mine, mine!" and again an awful laugh rang through the room. At the instant she turned. O the face of malign horror that met my gaze! The green eyes flamed, and with something like the snarl of a savage beast she sprang toward me; that hideous face almost touched mine; the grasp of the skinny jeweled hand was all but on me; then—I suppose I fainted.

For weeks I lay in brain fever, in mental horror and weariness so intent, that even now I do not like to let my mind dwell on it. Even when the crisis was safely past I was slow to rally; my mind was utterly unstrung. I lived in a world of shadows. And so winter wore by, and brought us to the fair spring morning when at last I stood by Robert's side in the old church, a cold, passive, almost unwilling bride. I cared neither to refuse nor consent to anything that was suggested; so Robert and Archie decided for me, and I allowed them to do with me as they would, while I brooded silently and ceaselessly on the memory of that terrible night. To my husband I told all one morning in a sunny Bavarian valley, and my weak, frightened mind drew strength and peace from his; by degrees the haunting horror wore away, and when we came home for a happy reason nearly two years afterward, I was as strong and blithe as in my girlhood. I had learned to believe that it had all been, not the cause, but the commencement of my fever. I was to be undeceived.

Our little daughter had come to us in the time of roses; and now Christmas was with us, our first Christmas at home, and the house was full of guests. It was a delicious old-fashioned Yule; plenty of skating and outdoor fun, and no lack of brightness indoors. Toward New Year a heavy fall of snow set in which kept us all prisoners; but even then the days flew merrily, and somebody suggested tableaux for the evenings. Robert was elected manager. There was a debate and selection of subjects, and then came the puzzle of where, at such short notice, we could procure the dresses required. My husband advised a raid on some mysterious oaken chests which he knew had been for years stowed away in a turret room. He remembered having, when a boy, seen the housekeeper inspecting them, and their contents had left a hazy impression of old stand-alone brocades, gold tissues, sacs, hoops, and hoods, the very mention of which put us in a state of wild excitement. Mrs. Moultrie was summoned, looked duly horrified at the desecration of what to her were relics most sacred; but seeing it was inevitable, she marshaled the way, a protest in every rustle and fold of her stiff silk dress.

"What a charming old place," was the exclamation with variations as we entered the long oak-joisted room, at the farther end of which stood in goodly array the chests whose contents we coveted. Bristling with unspoken disapproval, poor Mrs. Moultrie unlocked one after another, and then asked permission to retire, leaving us unchecked to "cry havoc." In a moment the floor was covered with piles of silks and velvets.

"Meg," cried little Janet Crawford, dancing up to me, "isn't it a good thing to live in the age of tulle and summer silks? Fancy being imprisoned for life in a fortress like this!" holding up a thick crimson and gold brocade, whale-boned and buckramed at all points. It was thrown aside, and she half lost herself in another chest and was silent. Then—"Look, Major Fraudel! This is the very thing for you—a true astrologer's robe, all black velvet and golden stars. If it were but long enough; it just fits me."

I turned and saw—the pretty slight figure, the innocent girlish face dressed in the robe of black and gold, identical in shape, pattern, and material with what I, too, well remembered. With a wild cry I hid my face and cowered away.

"Take it off! O, Janet—Robert—take it from her!"

Everyone turned wondering. In an instant my husband saw, and catching up the cause of my terror, flung it hastily into the chest again, and lowered the lid. Janet looked half offended, but the cloud passed in an instant when I kissed her, apologizing as well as I could. Rob laughed at us both, and voted an adjournment to a warmer room, where we could have the chests brought to us to ransack at leisure. Before going down, Janet and I went into a small anteroom to examine some old pictures which leaned against the wall.

"This is just the thing, Jennie, to frame the tableaux," I said, pointing to an immense frame, at least twelve feet square. "There is a picture in it," I added, pulling back the dusty folds of a heavy curtain which fell before it.

"That can be easily removed," said my husband, who had followed us.

With his assistance we drew the curtain quite away, and in the now fast waning light could just discern the figure of a girl in white against a dark background. Robert rang for a lamp, and when it came we turned with much curiosity to examine the painting, as to the subject of which we had been making odd merry guesses while we waited. The girl was young, almost childish—very lovely, but, oh, how sad! Great tears stood in the innocent eyes and on the round young cheeks, and her hands were clasped tenderly around the arms of a man who was bending toward her, and, did I dream?—No, there in hateful distinctness was the hideous woman of the Cedar Closet— the same in every distorted line, even to the starred dress and golden circlet. The swarthy hues of the dress and face had at first caused us to overlook her. The same wicked eyes seemed to glare into mine. After one wild bound my heart seemed to stop its beating, and I knew no more. When I recovered from a long, deep swoon, great lassitude and intense nervous excitement followed. My illness broke up the party, and for months I was an invalid. When again Robert's love and patience had won me back to my old health and happiness, he told me all the truth, so far as it had been preserved in old records of the family.

It was in the sixteenth century that the reigning lady of Draye Court was a weird, deformed woman, whose stunted body, hideous face, and a temper which taught

her to hate and vilify everything good and beautiful
for the contrast offered to herself, made her universally
feared and disliked. One talent only she possessed; it was
for music; but so wild and strange were the strains she
drew from the many instruments of which she was mistress, that the gift only intensified the dread with which
she was regarded. Her father had died before her birth.
Her mother did not survive it. Near relatives she had
none. She had lived her lonely, loveless life from youth to
middle age. When a young girl came to the Court, no one
knew more than that she was a poor relation. The dark
woman seemed to look more kindly on this young cousin
than on anyone that had hitherto crossed her somber
path, and indeed so great was the charm which Marian's
goodness, beauty, and innocent gaiety exercised on every
one that the servants ceased to marvel at her having
gained the favor of their gloomy mistress. The girl seemed
to feel a kind of wondering, pitying affection for the un-
happy woman; she looked on her through an atmosphere created by her own sunny nature, and for a time
all went well. When Marian had been at the Court for a
year, a foreign musician appeared on the scene. He was a
Spaniard, and had been engaged by Lady Draye to build
for her an organ said to be of fabulous power and sweetness. Through long bright summer days he and his em-
ployer were shut up together in the music room—he
busy in the construction of the wonderful instrument, she
aiding and watching his work. These days were spent by
Marian in various ways—pleasant idleness and pleasant
work, long canters on her chestnut pony, dreamy morn-
ings by the brook with rod and line, or in the village near,
where she found a welcome everywhere. She played with
the children, nursed the babies, helped the mothers in a

thousand pretty ways, gossiped with old people, brightening the day for everybody with whom she came in contact. Then in the evening she sat with Lady Draye and the Spaniard in the saloon talking in that soft foreign tongue which they generally used. But this was but the music between the acts; the terrible drama was coming. The motive was of course the same as that of every life drama which has been played out from the old, old days when the curtain rose upon the garden scene of Paradise. Philip and Marian loved each other, and having told their happy secret to each other, they, as in duty bound, took it to their patroness. They found her in the music room. Whether the glimpses she caught of a beautiful world from which she was shut out maddened her, or whether she, too, loved the foreigner, was never certainly known; but through the closed door passionate words were heard, and very soon Philip came out alone, and left the house without a farewell to any in it. When the servants did at last venture to enter, they found Marian lifeless on the floor, Lady Draye standing over her with crutch uplifted, and blood flowing from a wound in the girl's forehead. They carried her away and nursed her tenderly; their mistress locked the door as they left, and all night long remained alone in darkness. The music which came out without pause on the still night air was weird and wicked beyond any strains which had ever before flowed even from beneath her fingers. It ceased with morning light; and as the day wore on it was found that Marian had fled during the night, and that Philip's organ had sounded its last strain—Lady Draye had shattered and silenced it forever. She never seemed to notice Marian's absence and no one dared to mention her name. Nothing was ever known certainly of her fate; it was supposed that she had joined her lover.

Years passed, and with each Lady Draye's temper grew fiercer and more malevolent. She never quitted her room unless on the anniversary of that day and night, when the tapping of her crutch and high-heeled shoes was heard for hours as she walked up and down the music room, which was never entered save for this yearly vigil. The tenth anniversary came round, and this time the vigil was not unshared. The servants distinctly heard the sound of a man's voice mingling in earnest conversation with her shrill tones; they listened long, and at last one of the boldest ventured to look in, himself unseen. He saw a worn, travel-stained man; dusty, foot-sore, poorly dressed, he still at once recognized the handsome, gay Philip of ten years ago. He held in his arms a little sleeping girl; her long curls, so like poor Marian's, strayed over his shoulder. He seemed to be pleading in that strange musical tongue for the little one; for as he spoke he lifted, O, so tenderly, the cloak which partly concealed her, and showed the little face, which he doubtless thought might plead for itself. The woman, with a furious gesture, raised her crutch to strike the child. He stepped quickly backward, stooped to kiss the little girl, then, without a word, turned to go. Lady Draye called on him to return with an imperious gesture, spoke a few words, to which he seemed to listen gratefully, and together they left the house by the window which opened on the terrace. The servants followed them, and found she led the way to the parsonage, which was at the time unoccupied. It was said that he was in some political danger as well as in deep poverty, and that she had hidden him here until she could help him to a better asylum. It was certain that for many nights she went to the parsonage and returned before dawn, thinking herself unseen. But one morning she did not come home. Her people consulted together. Her relenting toward Philip had made them feel more kindly toward her than ever before. They sought her at the parsonage and found her lying across its threshold dead, a vial clasped in her rigid fingers. There was no sign of the late presence of Philip and his child; it was believed she had sped them on their way before she killed herself. They laid her in a suicide's grave. For more than fifty years after the parsonage was shut up. Though it had been again inhabited no one had ever been terrified by the specter I had seen; probably the Cedar Closet had never before been used as a bedroom.

Robert decided on having the wing containing the haunted room pulled down and rebuilt, and in doing so the truth of my story gained a horrible confirmation. When the wainscot of the Cedar Closet was removed a recess was discovered in the massive old wall, and in this lay moldering fragments of the skeletons of a man and a child!

There could be but one conclusion drawn, the wicked woman had imprisoned them there under pretense of hiding and helping them; and once they were completely at her mercy, had come night after night with unimaginable cruelty to gloat over their agony, and, when that long anguish was ended, ended her odious life by a suicide's death. We could learn nothing of the mysterious painting. Philip was an artist, and it may have been his work. We had it destroyed, so that no record of the terrible story might remain. I have no more to add, save that but for those dark days left by Lady Draye as a

legacy of fear and horror, I should never have known so
well the treasure I hold in the tender, unwearying, faithful
love of my husband—known the blessing that every sorrow carries in its heart, that

    "Every cloud that spreads above
    And veileth love, itself is love."

The Adventure of the German Student

Washington Irving
(1783–1859)

Dietrich Knickerbocker. Jonathan Oldstyle. Geoffrey Crayon. Best known today as Washington Irving. Short-story writer, essayist, poet, travel-book writer, biographer, columnist, he was our first great American writer. Born in New York City, he possessed charm, grace, and wit. From 1802 to 1814, he wrote for journals and newspapers, but in 1815, after the death of his fiancée, Irving sailed for Europe and remained there for seventeen years. During his time abroad he wrote several nonfiction works, all based on careful research, while working for the U.S. Embassy, then as secretary to the American Legation under Martin Van Buren. In 1832, he returned to New York, where he was welcomed as the first American writer to gain international fame. The theme of old Europe, quickly vanishing and mysterious, intrigued him, his appetite no doubt whetted by the extensive research he had engaged in while abroad. Old German folklore was his passion. His incomparable "Rip Van Winkle" and "The Legend of Sleepy Hollow" are both based on German tales, but transplanted to his home soil of New York. Most of his short stories, however, were set in Europe. "The Adventure of the German Student" takes place in old-charm Paris.

On a stormy night, in the tempestuous times of the French revolution, a young German was returning to his lodgings, at a late hour, across the old part of Paris. The lightning gleamed, and the loud claps of thunder rattled through the lofty narrow streets—but I should first tell you something about this young German.

Gottfried Wolfgang was a young man of good family. He had studied for some time at Göttingen, but being of a visionary and enthusiastic character, he had wandered into those wild and speculative doctrines which have so often bewildered German students. His secluded life, his intense application, and the singular nature of his studies had an effect on both mind and body. His health was impaired; his imagination diseased. He had been indulging in fanciful speculations on spiritual essences, until, like Swedenborg, he had an ideal world of his own around him. He took up a notion, I do not know from what cause, that there was an evil influence hanging over him; an evil genius or spirit seeking to ensnare him and ensure his perdition. Such an idea working on his melancholy temperament produced the most gloomy effects. He became haggard and desponding. His friends discovered the mental malady preying upon him, and determined that the best cure was a change of scene; he was sent, therefore, to finish his studies amidst the splendors and gaieties of Paris.

Wolfgang arrived at Paris at the breaking out of the revolution. The popular delirium at first caught his enthusiastic mind, and he was captivated by the political and philosophical theories of the day: but the scenes of blood which followed shocked his sensitive nature, disgusted him with society and the world, and made him more than ever a recluse. He shut himself up in a solitary apartment in the *Pays Latin*, the quarter of students. There, in a gloomy street not far from the monastic walls of the Sorbonne, he pursued his favorite speculations. Sometimes he spent hours together in the great libraries of Paris, those catacombs of departed authors, rummaging among their hordes of dusty and obsolete works in quest of food for his unhealthy appetite. He was, in a manner, a literary ghoul, feeding in the charnel house of decayed literature.

Wolfgang, though solitary and recluse, was of an ardent temperament, but for a time it operated merely upon his imagination. He was too shy and ignorant of the world to make any advances to the fair, but he was a passionate admirer of female beauty, and in his lonely chamber would often lose himself in reveries on forms and faces which he had seen, and his fancy would deck out images of loveliness far surpassing the reality.

While his mind was in this excited and sublimated state, a dream produced an extraordinary effect upon him. It was of a female face of transcendent beauty. So strong was the impression made that he dreamt of it again and again. It haunted his thoughts by day, his slumbers by night; in fine, he became passionately enamored of this shadow of a dream. This lasted so long that it became one of those fixed ideas which haunt the minds of melancholy men, and are at times mistaken for madness.

Such was Gottfried Wolfgang, and such his situation at the time I mentioned. He was returning home late one stormy night, through some of the old and gloomy streets of the *Marais,* the ancient part of Paris. The loud claps of thunder rattled among the high houses of the narrow streets. He came to the Place de Grève, the square where public executions are performed. The lightning quivered about the pinnacles of the ancient Hôtel de Ville, and shed flickering gleams over the open space in front. As Wolfgang was crossing the square, he shrank back with horror at finding himself close by the guillotine. It was the height of the reign of terror, when this dreadful instrument of death stood ever ready, and its scaffold was continually running with the blood of the virtuous and the brave. It had that very day been actively employed in the work of carnage, and there it stood in grim array, amidst a silent and sleeping city, waiting for fresh victims.

Wolfgang's heart sickened within him, and he was turning shuddering from the horrible engine, when he beheld a shadowy form, cowering as it were at the foot of the steps which led up to the scaffold. A succession of vivid flashes of lightning revealed it more distinctly. It was a female figure, dressed in black. She was seated on one of the lower steps of the scaffold, leaning forward, her face hid in her lap; and her long disheveled tresses hanging to the ground, streaming with the rain which fell in torrents. Wolfgang paused. There was something awful in this solitary monument of woe. The female had the appearance of being above the common order. He knew the times to be full of vicissitude, and that many a fair head, which had once been pillowed on down, now wandered houseless. Perhaps this was some poor mourner whom the dreadful axe had rendered desolate, and who sat here heartbroken on the strand of existence, from which all that was dear to her had been launched into eternity.

He approached, and addressed her in the accents of sympathy. She raised her head and gazed wildly at him. What was his astonishment at beholding, by the bright glare of the lightning, the very face which had haunted him in his dreams. It was pale and disconsolate, but ravishingly beautiful.

Trembling with violent and conflicting emotions, Wolfgang again accosted her. He spoke something of her being exposed at such an hour of the night, and to the fury of such a storm, and offered to conduct her to her friends. She pointed to the guillotine with a gesture of dreadful signification.

"I have no friend on earth!" said she.

"But you have a home," said Wolfgang.

"Yes—in the grave!"

The heart of the student melted at the words.

"If a stranger dare make an offer," said he, "without danger of being misunderstood, I would offer my humble dwelling as a shelter; myself as a devoted friend. I am friendless myself in Paris, and a stranger in the land; but if my life could be of service, it is at your disposal, and should be sacrificed before harm or indignity should come to you."

There was an honest earnestness in the young man's manner that had its effect. His foreign accent, too, was in his favor; it showed him not to be a hackneyed inhabitant of Paris. Indeed, there is an eloquence in true enthusiasm that is not to be doubted. The homeless stranger confided herself implicitly to the protection of the student.

He supported her faltering steps across the Pont Neuf, and by the place where the statue of Henry the Fourth had been overthrown by the populace. The storm had abated, and the thunder rumbled at a distance. All Paris was quiet, that great volcano of human passion slumbered for a while, to gather fresh strength for the next day's eruption. The student conducted his charge through the ancient streets of the *Pays Latin*, and by the dusky walls of the Sorbonne, to the great dingy hotel which he inhabited. The old portress who admitted them stared with surprise at the unusual sight of the melancholy Wolfgang with a female companion.

On entering his apartment, the student, for the first time, blushed at the scantiness and indifference of his dwelling. He had but one chamber—an old-fashioned saloon—heavily carved, and fantastically furnished with the remains of former magnificence, for it was one of those hotels in the quarter of the Luxembourg palace which had once belonged to nobility. It was lumbered with books and papers, and all the usual apparatus of a student, and his bed stood in a recess at one end.

When lights were brought, and Wolfgang had a better opportunity of contemplating the stranger, he was more than ever intoxicated by her beauty. Her face was pale, but of a dazzling fairness, set off by a profusion of raven hair that hung clustering about it. Her eyes were large and brilliant, with a singular expression approaching almost to wildness. As far as her black dress permitted her shape to be seen, it was of perfect symmetry. Her whole appearance was highly striking, though she was dressed in the simplest style. The only thing approaching to an ornament which she wore, was a broad black band round her neck, clasped by diamonds.

The perplexity now commenced with the student how to dispose of the helpless being thus thrown upon his protection. He thought of abandoning his chamber to her, and seeking shelter for himself elsewhere. Still he was so fascinated by her charms, there seemed to be such a spell upon his thoughts and senses, that he could not tear himself from her presence. Her manner, too, was singular and unaccountable. She spoke no more of the guillotine. Her grief had abated. The attentions of the student had first won her confidence, and then, apparently, her heart. She was evidently an enthusiast like himself, and enthusiasts soon understand each other.

In the infatuation of the moment, Wolfgang avowed his passion for her. He told her the story of his mysterious dream, and how she had possessed his heart before he had even seen her. She was strangely affected by his recital, and acknowledged to have felt an impulse toward him equally unaccountable. It was the time for wild theory and wild actions. Old prejudices and superstitions were done away; everything was under the sway of the "Goddess of Reason." Among other rubbish of the old times, the forms and ceremonies of marriage began to be considered superfluous bonds for honorable minds. Social compacts were the vogue. Wolfgang was too much of a theorist not to be tainted by the liberal doctrines of the day.

"Why should we separate?" said he; "our hearts are united; in the eye of reason and honor we are as one. What need is there of sordid forms to bind high souls together?"

The stranger listened with emotion; she had evidently received illumination at the same school.

"You have no home or family," continued he, "let me be everything to you, or rather let us be everything to one another. If form is necessary, form shall be observed—there is my hand. I pledge myself to you forever."

"Forever?" said the stranger, solemnly.

"Forever!" repeated Wolfgang.

The stranger clasped the hand extended to her: "Then I am yours," murmured she, and sank upon his bosom.

The next morning the student left his bride sleeping, and sallied forth at an early hour to seek more spacious apartments suitable to the change in his situation. When he returned, he found the stranger lying with her head hanging over the bed, and one arm thrown over it. He spoke to her, but received no reply. He advanced to awaken her from her uneasy posture. On taking her hand, it was cold—there was no pulsation—her face was pallid and ghastly. In a word, she was a corpse.

Horrified and frantic, he alarmed the house. A sense of confusion ensued. The police were summoned. As the officer of police entered the room, he started back on beholding the corpse.

"Great Heaven!" cried he. "How did this woman come here?"

"Do you know anything about her?" said Wolfgang eagerly.

"Do I?" exclaimed the officer: "She was guillotined yesterday."

He stepped forward; undid the black collar round the neck of the corpse, and the head rolled on the floor!

The student burst into a frenzy. "The fiend! The fiend has gained possession of me!" shrieked he; "I am lost forever."

They tried to soothe him, but in vain. He was possessed with the frightful belief that an evil spirit had reanimated the dead body to ensnare him. He went distracted, and died in a madhouse.

Here the old gentleman with the haunted head finished his narrative.

"And is this really a fact?" said the inquisitive gentleman.

"A fact not to be doubted," replied the other. "I had it from the best authority. The student told it me himself. I saw him in a madhouse in Paris."

The Lost Room

Fitz-James O'Brien
(1828–1862)

Born in County Limerick, Ireland, Fitz-James O'Brien was an only
child to whom his father left a significant inheritance upon his
death. He was remarkably productive as a writer, publishing
poems, stories, and articles in a variety of Irish, Scottish, and
English periodicals. In 1852, he emigrated to the United States
and became a welcomed and esteemed member of the Bohemian
circles of New York City. It is said that O'Brien was well educated
in the use of sword and revolver, the finest weapons the day's
technology could offer. In the 1850s, he wrote fantasies, dream
stories, and ghost stories. During this decade, he also wrote plays,
which were so popular that their songs were performed throughout
New York City. As the Civil War became imminent, his patriotism
for his new homeland moved him to leave his literary circle and
volunteer with the Union army. Of course, he worked his pen
during these trying times, and his poems of the Civil War are
considered among the best. Sadly, he died of an infected wound
several weeks after he was shot in the shoulder during the Battle of
Bloomery Gap. O'Brien helped shape the short story at a time
when the literary magazine was a new medium, successfully
reaching a broad audience. Some of O'Brien's writings are
considered the precursors of science fiction. For *One Dark Night* I
chose a ghastly nightmare called "The Lost Room." Cannibalistic
thieves invade their neighbor's room and transform the worldly
man's beloved and sentimental possessions to create their own
den of Hell. O'Brien's details are haunting.

*I*t was oppressively warm. The sun had long disappeared, but seemed to have left its vital spirit of heat behind it. The air rested; the leaves of the acacia trees that shrouded my windows hung plumb-like on their delicate stalks. The smoke of my cigar scarce rose above my head, but hung about me in a pale blue cloud, which I had to dissipate with languid waves of my hand. My shirt was open at the throat, and my chest heaved laboriously in the effort to catch some breaths of fresher air. The noises of the city seemed to be wrapped in slumber, and the shrilling of the mosquitoes was the only sound that broke the stillness.

As I lay with my feet elevated on the back of a chair, wrapped in that peculiar frame of mind in which thought assumes a species of lifeless motion, the strange fancy seized me of making a languid inventory of the principal articles of furniture in my room. It was a task well suited to the mood in which I found myself. Their forms were duskily defined in the dim twilight that floated shadowily through the chamber; it was no labor to note and particularize each, and from the place where I sat I could command a view of all my possessions without even turning my head.

There was, *imprimis,* that ghostly lithograph by Calame. It was a mere black spot on the white wall, but

my inner vision scrutinized every detail of the picture. A
wild, desolate, midnight heath, with a spectral oak tree in
the center of the foreground. The wind blows fiercely,
and the jagged branches, clothed scantily with ill-grown
leaves, are swept to the left continually by its giant force.
A formless wrack of clouds streams across the awful sky,
and the rain sweeps almost parallel with the horizon. Beyond, the heath stretches off into endless blackness, in
the extreme of which either fancy or art has conjured up
some undefinable shapes that seem riding into space. At
the base of the huge oak stands a shrouded figure. His
mantle is wound by the blast in tight folds around his
form, and the long cock's feather in his hat is blown upright, till it seems as if it stood on end with fear. His features are not visible, for he has grasped his cloak with
both hands, and drawn it from either side across his face.
The picture is seemingly objectless. It tells no tale, but
there is a weird power about it that haunts one.

Next to the picture comes the round blot that hangs
below it, which I know to be a smoking cap. It has my
coat of arms embroidered on the front, and for that reason I never wear it; though, when properly arranged on
my head, with its long blue silken tassel hanging down
by my cheek, I believe it becomes me well. I remember
the time when it was in the course of manufacture. I remember the tiny little hands that pushed the colored silks
so nimbly through the cloth that was stretched on the
embroidery frame—the vast trouble I was put to get a
colored copy of my armorial bearings for the heraldic
work which was to decorate the front of the band—the
pursings up of the little mouth, and the contractions of
the young forehead, as their possessor plunged into a
profound sea of cogitation touching the way in which the

cloud should be represented from which the armed hand, that is my crest, issues—the heavenly moment when the tiny hands placed it on my head, in a position that I could not bear for more than a few seconds, and I, king-like, immediately assumed my royal prerogative after the coronation, and instantly levied a tax on my only subject, which was, however, not paid unwillingly. Ah, the cap is there, but the embroiderer has fled; for Atropos was severing the web of life above her head while she was weaving that silken shelter for mine!

How uncouthly the huge piano that occupies the corner at the left of the door looms out in the uncertain twilight! I neither play nor sing, yet I own a piano. It is a comfort to me to look at it, and to feel that the music is there, although I am not able to break the spell that binds it. It is pleasant to know that Bellini and Mozart, Cimarosa, Porpora, Gluck, and all such—or at least their souls—sleep in that unwieldy case. There lie embalmed, as it were, all operas, sonatas, oratorios, notturnos, marches, songs, and dances, that ever climbed into existence through the four bars that wall in a melody. Once I was entirely repaid for the investment of my funds in that instrument which I never use. Blokeeta, the composer, came to see me. Of course his instincts urged him as irresistibly to my piano as if some magnetic power lay within it compelling him to approach. He tuned it, he played on it. All night long, until the gray and spectral dawn rose out of the depths of the midnight, he sat and played, and I lay smoking by the window listening. Wild, unearthly, and sometimes insufferably painful, were the improvisations of Blokeeta. The chords of the instrument seemed breaking with anguish. Lost souls shrieked in his dismal preludes; the half-heard utterances of spirits in pain, that groped at inconceivable distances from anything lovely or harmonious, seemed to rise dimly up out of the waves of sound that gathered under his hands. Melancholy human love wandered out on distant heaths, or beneath dank and gloomy cypresses, murmuring its unanswered sorrow, or hateful gnomes sported and sang in the stagnant swamps, triumphing in unearthly tones over the knight whom they had lured to his death. Such was Blokeeta's night's entertainment; and when he at length closed the piano, and hurried away through the cold morning, he left a memory about the instrument from which I could never escape.

Those snowshoes that hang in the space between the mirror and the door recall Canadian wanderings—a long race through the dense forests, over the frozen snow, through whose brittle crust the slender hoofs of the caribou that we were pursuing sank at every step, until the poor creature despairingly turned at bay in a small juniper coppice, and we heartlessly shot him down. And I remember how Gabriel, the *habitant*, and François, the halfbreed, cut his throat, and how the hot blood rushed out in a torrent over the snowy soil; and I recall the snow *cabane* that Gabriel built, where we all three slept so warmly; and the great fire that glowed at our feet, painting all kinds of demoniac shapes on the black screen of forest that lay without; and the deer steaks that we roasted for our breakfast; and the savage drunkenness of Gabriel in the morning, he having been privately drinking out of my brandy flask all the night long.

That long, haftless dagger that dangles over the mantelpiece makes my heart swell. I found it, when a boy, in a hoary old castle in which one of my maternal ancestors once lived. That same ancestor—who, by the way, yet lives in history—was a strange old sea-king, who dwelt on the extremest point of the southwestern coast of Ireland. He owned the whole of that fertile island called Inniskei-ran, which directly faces Cape Clear, where between them the Atlantic rolls furiously, forming what the fishermen of the place call "the Sound." An awful place in winter is that same Sound. On certain days no boat can live there for a moment, and Cape Clear is frequently cut off for days from any communication with the mainland.

This old sea-king—Sir Florence O'Driscoll by name—passed a stormy life. From the summit of his castle he watched the ocean, and when any richly laden vessels, bound from the south to the industrious Galway merchants, hove in sight, Sir Florence hoisted the sails of his galley, and it went hard with him if he did not tow into harbor ship and crew. In this way, he lived; not a very honest mode of livelihood, certainly, according to our modern ideas, but quite reconcilable with the morals of the time. As may be supposed, Sir Florence got into trouble. Complaints were laid against him at the English court by the plundered merchants, and the Irish viking set out for London, to plead his own cause before good Queen Bess, as she was called. He had one powerful recommendation: he was a marvelously handsome man. Not Celtic by descent, but half Spanish, half Danish in blood, he had the great northern stature with the regular features, flashing eyes, and dark hair of the Iberian race. This may account for the fact that his stay at the English court was much longer than was necessary, as also for the tradition, which a local historian mentions, that the English Queen evinced a preference for the Irish chieftain, of other nature than that usually shown by monarch to subject.

Previous to his departure, Sir Florence had entrusted the care of his property to an Englishman named Hull. During the long absence of the knight, this person managed to ingratiate himself with the local authorities, and gain their favor so far that they were willing to support him in almost any scheme. After a protracted stay, Sir Florence, pardoned of all his misdeeds, returned to his home. Home no longer. Hull was in possession, and refused to yield an acre of the lands he had so nefariously acquired. It was no use appealing to the law, for its officers were in the opposite interest. It was no use appealing to the Queen, for she had another lover, and had forgotten the poor Irish knight by this time; and so the viking passed the best portion of his life in unsuccessful attempts to reclaim his vast estates, and was eventually, in his old age, obliged to content himself with his castle by the sea and the island of Inniskeiran, the only spot of which the usurper was unable to deprive him. So this old story of my kinsman's fate looms up out of the darkness that enshrouds that haftless dagger hanging on the wall.

It was somewhat after the foregoing fashion that I dreamily made the inventory of my personal property. As I turned my eyes on each object, one after the other—or the places where they lay, for the room was now so dark that it was almost impossible to see with any distinctness—a crowd of memories connected with each rose up before me, and, perforce, I had to indulge them. So I proceeded but slowly, and at last my cigar shortened to a hot and bitter morsel that I could barely hold between my lips, while it seemed to me that the night grew each moment more insufferably oppressive. While I was revolving some impossible means of cooling my wretched body, the cigar stump began to burn my lips. I flung it angrily through the open window, and stooped out to watch it falling. It first lighted on the leaves of the acacia, sending out a spray of red sparkles, then, rolling off, it fell plump on the dark walk in the garden, faintly illuminating for a moment the dusky trees and breathless flowers. Whether it was the contrast between the red flash of the cigar stump and the silent darkness of the garden, or whether it was that I detected by the sudden light a faint waving of the leaves, I know not; but something suggested to me that the garden was cool. I will take a turn there, thought I, just as I am; it cannot be warmer than this room, and however still the atmosphere, there is always a feeling of liberty and spaciousness in the open air that partially supplies one's wants. With this idea running through my head, I arose, lit another cigar, and passed out into the long, intricate corridors that led to the main staircase. As I crossed the threshold of my room, with what a different feeling I should have passed it had I known that I was never to set foot in it again!

I lived in a very large house, in which I occupied two rooms on the second floor. The house was old-fashioned, and all the floors communicated by a huge circular staircase that wound up through the center of the building, while at every landing long, rambling corridors stretched off into mysterious nooks and corners. This palace of mine was very high, and its resources, in the way of crannies and windings, seemed to be interminable. Nothing seemed to stop anywhere. Cul-de-sacs were unknown on the premises. The corridors and passages, like mathematical lines, seemed capable of indefinite extensions, and the object of the architect must have been to erect an edifice in which people might go ahead forever. The whole place was gloomy, not so much because it was large, but because an unearthly nakedness seemed to pervade the structure. The staircases, corridors, halls, and vestibules all partook of a desert-like desolation. There was nothing on the walls to break the somber monotony of those long vistas of shade. No carvings on the wain-scoting, no molded masks peering down from the simply severe cornices, no marble vases on the landings. There was an eminent dreariness and want of life—so rare in an American establishment—all over the abode. It was Hood's haunted house put in order and newly painted. The servants, too, were shadowy, and chary of their visits. Bells rang three times before the gloomy chamber-maid could be induced to present herself; and the Negro waiter, a ghoul-like-looking creature from the Congo, obeyed the summons only when one's patience was exhausted or one's want satisfied in some other way. When he did come, one felt sorry that he had not stayed away altogether, so sullen and savage did he appear. He moved along the echoless floors with a slow, noiseless shamble, until his dusky figure, advancing from the gloom, seemed like some reluctant afreet, compelled by the superior power of his master to disclose himself. When the doors of all the chambers were closed, and no light illuminated the long corridor save the red, unwholesome glare of a small oil lamp on a table at the end, where late lodgers lit their candles, one could not by any possibility conjure up a sadder or more desolate prospect.

Yet the house suited me. Of meditative and sedentary habits, I enjoyed the extreme quiet. There were but few lodgers, from which I infer that the landlord did not drive a very thriving trade; and these, probably oppressed by the somber spirit of the place, were quiet and ghost-like in their movements. The proprietor I scarcely ever saw.

My bills were deposited by unseen hands every month on my table, while I was out walking or riding, and my pecuniary response was entrusted to the attendant afreet. On the whole, when the bustling wide-awake spirit of New York is taken into consideration, the somber, half-vivified character of the house in which I lived was an anomaly that no one appreciated better than I who lived there.

I felt my way down the wide, dark staircase in my pursuit of zephyrs. The garden, as I entered it, did feel somewhat cooler than my own room, and I puffed my cigar along the dim, cypress-shrouded walks with a sensation of comparative relief. It was very dark. The tall-growing flowers that bordered the path were so wrapped in gloom as to present the aspect of solid pyramidal masses, all the details of leaves and blossoms being buried in an embracing darkness, while the trees had lost all form, and seemed like masses of overhanging cloud. It was a place and time to excite the imagination; for in the impenetrable cavities of endless gloom there was room for the most riotous fancies to play at will. I walked and walked, and the echoes of my footsteps on the ungraveled and mossy path suggested a double feeling. I felt alone and yet in company at the same time. The solitariness of the place made itself distinct enough in the stillness, broken alone by the hollow reverberations of my step, while those very reverberations seemed to imbue me with an undefined feeling that I was not alone. I was not, therefore, much startled when I was suddenly accosted from beneath the solid darkness of an immense cypress by a voice saying, "Will you give me a light, sir?"

"Certainly," I replied, trying in vain to distinguish the speaker amidst the impenetrable dark.

Somebody advanced, and I held out my cigar. All I could gather definitely about the individual who thus accosted me was that he must have been of extremely small stature; for I, who am by no means an overgrown man, had to stoop considerably in handing him my cigar. The vigorous puff that he gave his own lighted up my Havana for a moment, and I fancied that I caught a glimpse of a pale, weird countenance, immersed in a background of long, wild hair. The flash was, however, so momentary that I could not even say certainly whether this was an actual impression or the mere effort of imagination to embody that which the senses had failed to distinguish.

"Sir, you are out late," said this unknown to me, as he, with half-uttered thanks, handed me back my cigar, for which I had to grope in the gloom.

"Not later than usual," I replied, dryly.

"Hum! You are fond of late wanderings, then?"

"That is just as the fancy seizes me."

"Do you live here?"

"Yes."

"Queer house, isn't it?"

"I have only found it quiet."

"Hum! But you *will* find it queer, take my word for it." This was earnestly uttered; and I felt at the same time a bony finger laid on my arm, that cut it sharply like a blunted knife.

"I cannot take your word for any such assertion," I replied, rudely, shaking off the bony finger with an irrepressible motion of disgust.

"No offense, no offense," muttered my unseen companion rapidly, in a strange, subdued voice that would have been shrill had it been louder; "your being angry does not alter the matter. You will find it a queer house. Everybody finds it a queer house. Do you know who lives there?"

"I never busy myself, sir, about other people's affairs," I answered sharply, for the individual's manner, combined with my utter uncertainty as to his appearance, oppressed me with an irksome longing to be rid of him.

"O, you don't? Well, I do. I know what they are—well, well, well!" and as he pronounced the three last words his voice rose with each, until, with the last, it reached a shrill shriek that echoed horribly among the lonely walks. "Do you know what they eat?" he continued.

"No, sir—nor care."

"O, but you will care. You must care. You shall care. I'll tell you what they are. They are enchanters. They are ghouls. They are cannibals. Did you never remark their eyes, and how they gloated on you when you passed? Did you never remark the food that they served up at your table? Did you never in the dead of night hear muffled and unearthly footsteps gliding along the corridors, and stealthy hands turning the handle of your door? Does not some magnetic influence fold itself continually around you when they pass, and send a thrill through spirit and body, and a cold shiver that no sunshine will chase away? O, you have! You have felt all these things! I know it!"

The earnest rapidity, the subdued tones, the eagerness of accent, with which all this was uttered, impressed me most uncomfortably. It really seemed as if I could recall all those weird occurrences and influences of which he spoke; and I shuddered in spite of myself in the midst of the impenetrable darkness that surrounded me.

"Hum!" said I, assuming, without knowing it, a confidential tone, "may I ask how you know these things?"

"How I know them? Because I am their enemy; because they tremble at my whisper; because I follow upon their track with the perseverance of a bloodhound and the stealthiness of a tiger; because—because—I was *of* them once!"

"Wretch!" I cried excitedly, for involuntarily his eager tones had wrought me up to a high pitch of spasmodic nervousness. "Then you mean to say that you—"

As I uttered this word, obeying an uncontrollable impulse, I stretched forth my hand in the direction of the speaker and made a blind clutch. The tips of my fingers seemed to touch a surface as smooth as glass, that glided suddenly from under them. A sharp, angry hiss sounded through the gloom, followed by a whirring noise, as if some projectile passed rapidly by, and the next moment I felt instinctively that I was alone.

A most disagreeable feeling instantly assailed me—a prophetic instinct that some terrible misfortune menaced me; an eager and overpowering anxiety to get back to my own room without loss of time. I turned and ran blindly along the dark cypress alley, every dusky clump of flowers that rose blackly in the borders making my heart each moment cease to beat. The echoes of my own footsteps seemed to redouble and assume the sounds of unknown pursuers following fast upon my track. The boughs of lilac bushes and syringas, that here and there stretched partly across the walk, seemed to have been furnished suddenly with hooked hands that sought to grasp me as I flew by, and each moment I expected to behold some awful and impassable barrier fall across my track and wall me up forever.

At length I reached the wide entrance. With a single leap I sprang up the four or five steps that formed the

stoop, and dashed along the hall, up the wide, echoing stairs, and again along the dim, funereal corridors
until I paused, breathless and panting, at the door of my
room. Once so far, I stopped for an instant and leaned
heavily against one of the panels, panting lustily after my
late run. I had, however, scarcely rested my whole weight
against the door, when it suddenly gave way, and I staggered in headforemost. To my utter astonishment the
room I had left in profound darkness was now a blaze
of light. So intense was the illumination that, for a few
seconds while the pupils of my eyes were contracting
under the sudden change, I saw absolutely nothing save
the dazzling glare. This fact in itself, coming on me with
such utter suddenness, was sufficient to prolong my confusion, and it was not until after several minutes had
elapsed that I perceived the room was not only illuminated, but occupied. And such occupants! Amazement at
the scene took such possession of me that I was incapable of either moving or uttering a word. All that I could
do was to lean against the wall, and stare blankly at the
strange picture.

It might have been a scene out of Faublas, or Gram-
mont's Memoirs, or happened in some palace of Minister
Fouqué.

Round a large table in the center of the room, where
I had left a studentlike litter of books and papers, were
seated a half a dozen persons. Three were men and three
were women. The table was heaped with a prodigality
of luxuries. Luscious eastern fruits were piled up in silver filigree vases, through whose meshes their glowing
rinds shone in the contrasts of a thousand hues. Small
silver dishes that Benvenuto might have designed, filled
with succulent and aromatic meats, were distributed upon

a cloth of snowy damask. Bottles of every shape, slender ones from the Rhine, stout fellows from Holland, sturdy ones from Spain, and quaint basket-woven flasks from Italy, absolutely littered the board. Drinking glasses of every size and hue filled up the interstices, and the thirsty German flagon stood side by side with the aerial bubbles of Venetian glass that rest so lightly on their threadlike stems. An odor of luxury and sensuality floated through the apartment. The lamps that burned in every direction seemed to diffuse a subtle incense on the air, and in a large vase that stood on the floor I saw a mass of magnolias, tuberoses, and jasmines grouped together, stifling each other with their honeyed and heavy fragrance.

The inhabitants of my room seemed beings well suited to so sensual an atmosphere. The women were strangely beautiful, and all were attired in dresses of the most fantastic devices and brilliant hues. Their figures were round, supple, and elastic; their eyes dark and languishing; their lips full, ripe, and of the richest bloom. The three men wore half masks, so that all I could distinguish were heavy jaws, pointed beards, and brawny throats that rose like massive pillars out of their doublets. All six lay reclining on Roman couches about the table, drinking down the purple wines in large drafts, and tossing back their heads and laughing wildly.

I stood, I suppose, for some three minutes, with my back against the wall staring vacantly at the bacchanal vision, before any of the revelers appeared to notice my presence. At length, without any expression to indicate whether I had been observed from the beginning or not, two of the women arose from their couches, and, approaching, took each a hand and led me to the table. I

obeyed their motions mechanically. I sat on a couch between them as they indicated. I unresistingly permitted
them to wind their arms about my neck.

"You must drink," said one, pouring out a large glass
of red wine; "here is Clos Vougeot of a rare vintage; and
here," pushing a flask of amber-hued wine before me, "is
Lachryma Christi."

"You must eat," said the other, drawing the silver
dishes toward her. "Here are cutlets stewed with olives,
and here are slices of a *filet* stuffed with bruised sweet
chestnuts"—and as she spoke, she, without waiting for a
reply, proceeded to help me.

The sight of the food recalled to me the warnings I
had received in the garden. This sudden effort of memory
restored to me my other faculties at the same instant. I
sprang to my feet, thrusting the women from me with
each hand.

"Demons!" I almost shouted. "I will have none of
your accursed food. I know you. You are cannibals, you
are ghouls, you are enchanters. Begone, I tell you! Leave
my room in peace!"

A shout of laughter from all six was the only effect
that my passionate speech produced. The men rolled on
their couches, and their half masks quivered with the
convulsions of their mirth. The women shrieked, and
tossed the slender wineglasses wildly aloft, and turned to
me and flung themselves on my bosom fairly sobbing
with laughter.

"Yes," I continued, as soon as the noisy mirth had
subsided, "yes, I say, leave my room instantly! I will have
none of your unnatural orgies here!"

"His room!" shrieked the woman on my right.

"His room!" echoed she on my left.

"His room! He calls it his room!" shouted the whole party, as they rolled once more into jocular convulsions.

"How know you that it is your room?" said one of the men who sat opposite to me, at length, after the laughter had once more somewhat subsided.

"How do I know?" I replied, indignantly. "How do I know my own room? How could I mistake it, pray? There's my furniture—my piano—"

"He calls that a piano!" shouted my neighbors.

The peculiar emphasis they laid on the word "piano" caused me to scrutinize the article I was indicating more thoroughly. Up to this time, though utterly amazed at the entrance of these people into my chamber, and connecting them somewhat with the wild stories I had heard in the garden, I still had a sort of indefinite idea that the whole thing was a masquerading freak got up in my absence, and that the bacchanalian orgy I was witnessing was nothing more than a portion of some elaborate hoax of which I was to be the victim. But when my eyes turned to the corner where I had left a huge and cumbrous piano, and beheld a vast and somber organ lifting its fluted front to the very ceiling, and convinced myself, by a hurried process of memory, that it occupied the very spot in which I had left my own instrument, the little self-possession that I had left forsook me. I gazed around me bewildered.

In like manner everything was changed. In the place of that old haftless dagger, connected with so many historic associations personal to myself, I beheld a Turkish yataghan dangling by its belt of crimson silk, while the jewels in the hilt blazed as the lamplight played upon them. In the spot where hung my cherished smoking-cap, memorial of a buried love, a knightly casque was suspended, on the crest of which a golden dragon stood in the act of springing. That strange lithograph by Calame was no longer a lithograph, but it seemed to me that the portion of the wall which it had covered, of the exact shape and size, had been cut out, and, in place of the picture, a *real* scene on the same scale, and with real actors, was distinctly visible. The old oak was there, and the stormy sky was there; but I saw the branches of the oak sway with the tempest, and the clouds drive before the wind. The wanderer in his cloak was gone; but in his place I beheld a circle of wild figures, men and women, dancing with linked hands around the bole of the great tree, chanting some wild fragment of a song, to which the winds roared an unearthly chorus. The snowshoes, too, on whose sinewy woof I had sped for many days amidst Canadian wastes, had vanished, and in their place lay a pair of strange upcurled Turkish slippers.

All was changed. Wherever my eyes turned they missed familiar objects, yet encountered strange representatives. Still, in all the substitutes there seemed to me a reminiscence of what they replaced. They seemed only for a time transmuted into other shapes, and there lingered around them the atmosphere of what they once had been. Thus I could have sworn the room to have been mine, yet there was nothing in it that I could rightly claim.

"Well, have you determined whether or not this is your room?" asked the girl on my left, proffering me a huge tumbler creaming over with champagne, and laughing wickedly as she spoke.

"It is mine," I answered, doggedly, striking the glass rudely with my hand, and dashing the aromatic wine over the white cloth.

"Hush! Hush!" she said, gently, not in the least angered at my rough treatment. "You are excited. Alf shall play something to soothe you."

At her signal, one of the men sat down at the organ. After a short, wild, spasmodic prelude, he began what seemed to me to be a symphony of recollections. Dark and somber, and all through full of quivering and intense agony, it appeared to recall a dark and dismal night, on a cold reef, around which an unseen but terribly audible ocean broke with eternal fury. It seemed as if a lonely pair were on the reef, one living, the other dead; one clasping his arms around the tender neck and naked bosom of the other, striving to warm her into life, when his own vitality was being each moment sucked from him by the icy breath of the storm. Here and there a terrible wailing minor key would tremble through the chords like the shriek of seabirds, or the warning of advancing death. While the man played I could scarce restrain myself. It seemed to be Blokeeta whom I listened to, and on whom I gazed. That wondrous night of pleasure and pain that I had once passed listening to him seemed to have been taken up again at the spot where it had broken off, and the same hand was continuing it. I stared at the man called Alf. There he sat with his cloak and doublet, and long rapier and mask of black velvet. But there was something in the air of the peaked beard, a familiar mystery in the wild mass of raven hair that fell as if windblown over his shoulders, which riveted my memory.

"Blokeeta! Blokeeta!" I shouted, starting up furiously

from the couch on which I was lying, and bursting the fair arms that were linked around my neck as if they had been hateful chains—"Blokeeta! My friend! Speak to me, I entreat you! Tell these horrid enchanters to leave me. Say that I hate them. Say that I command them to leave my room."

The man at the organ stirred not in answer to my appeal. He ceased playing, and the dying sound of the last note he had touched faded off into a melancholy moan.

"Why will you persist in calling this your room?" said the woman next to me, with a smile meant to be kind, but to me inexpressibly loathsome. "Have we not shown you by the furniture, by the general appearance of the place, that you are mistaken, and that this cannot be your apartment? Rest content, then, with us."

"Rest content?" I answered, madly. "Live with ghosts! Eat of awful meats, and see awful sights! Never, never!"

"Softly, softly!" said another of the sirens. "Let us settle this amicably. This poor gentleman seems obstinate and inclined to make an uproar.

"Now," she continued, "I have a proposition to make. It would be ridiculous for us to surrender this room simply because this gentleman states that it is his; and yet I feel anxious to gratify, as far as may be fair, his wild assertion of ownership. A room, after all, is not much to us; we can get one easily enough, but still we should be loath to give this apartment up to so imperious a demand. We are willing, however, to *risk* its loss. That is to say"—turning to me—"I propose that we play for the room. If you win, we will immediately surrender it to you just as it stands; if, on the contrary, you lose, you shall bind yourself to depart."

Agonized at the ever-darkening mysteries that seemed to thicken around me, and despairing of being able to dissipate them by the mere exercise of my own will, I caught almost gladly at the chance thus presented to me.

"I agree," I cried, eagerly; "I agree. Anything to rid myself of such unearthly company!"

The woman touched a small golden bell that stood near her on the table, and it had scarce ceased to tinkle when a Negro dwarf entered with a silver tray on which were dice boxes and dice. A shudder passed over me as I thought in this stunted African I could trace a resemblance to the ghoul-like black servant to whose attendance I had been accustomed.

"Now," said my neighbor, seizing one of the dice boxes and giving me the other, "the highest wins. Shall I throw first?"

I nodded assent. She rattled the dice, and I felt an inexpressible load lifted from my heart as she threw fifteen.

"It is your turn," she said, with a mocking smile; "but before you throw, I repeat the offer I made you before. Live with us. Be one of us."

My reply was a fierce oath, as I rattled the dice with spasmodic nervousness and flung them on the board. They rolled over and over again, and during that brief instant I felt a suspense, the intensity of which I have never known before or since. At last they lay before me. A shout of the same horrible, maddening laughter rang in my ears. I peered in vain at the dice, but my sight was so confused that I could not distinguish the amount of the cast. This lasted for a few moments. Then my sight grew clear, and I sank back almost lifeless with despair as I saw that I had thrown but *twelve!*

"Lost! Lost!" screamed my neighbor, with a wild laugh. "Lost! Lost!" shouted the deep voices of the masked men. "Leave us, coward!" they all cried. "You are not fit to be one of us. Remember your promise; leave us!"

Then it seemed as if some unseen power caught me by the shoulders and thrust me toward the door. In vain I resisted. In vain I screamed and shouted for help. In vain I screamed and twisted in despair. In vain I implored them for pity. All the reply I had was those mocking peals of merriment, while, under the invisible influence, I staggered like a drunken man toward the door. As I reached the threshold the organ pealed out a wild, triumphal strain. The power that impelled me concentrated itself into one vigorous impulse that sent me blindly staggering out into the echoing corridor, and, as the door closed swiftly behind me, I caught one glimpse of the apartment I had left forever. A change passed like a shadow over it. The lamps died out, the siren women and masked men had vanished, the flowers, the fruits, the bright silver and bizarre furniture faded swiftly, and I saw again, for the tenth of a second, my own old chamber restored.

The next instant the door closed violently, and I was left standing in the corridor stunned and despairing.

As soon as I had partially recovered my comprehension I rushed madly to the door, with the dim idea of beating it in. My fingers touched a cold and solid wall. There was no door! I felt all along the corridor for many yards on both sides. There was not even a crevice to give me hope. No one answered. In the vestibule I met the Negro. I seized him by the collar, and demanded my room. The demon showed his white and awful teeth, which were filed into a saw-like shape, and, extricating himself from my grasp with a sudden jerk, fled down the passage with a gibbering laugh. Nothing but echo answered to my despairing shrieks.

Since that awful hour I have never found my room. Everywhere I look for it, yet never see it. Shall I ever find it?

An Occurrence at Owl Creek Bridge (Excerpt)

Ambrose Bierce
(1842–1914?)

Author of the popular *The Devil's Dictionary*, in which he opens a Pandora's box of biting satirical aphorisms, Ambrose Bierce had an acid wit that earned him the moniker "Bitter Bierce." At the age of seventeen, he attended the Kentucky Military Institute at his father's insistence. The knowledge he gained there in map reading and army tactics served him well when he enlisted to fight in the Civil War. The war seared his understanding of death and dying, and as a young twenty-three-year-old writer, he was able to transfer the horrific images of battle onto paper with remarkable clarity and sensitivity. Many critics believe his war stories outrank those of Stephen Crane and Ernest Hemingway. After the war, he wrote prolifically, amassing more than a thousand newspaper columns and ninety-three short stories. Fifty-three of those stories are what we would consider "supernatural" today. Some biographers suspect that Bierce found writing necessary to keep his sanity, a method of sorting out the impact of the Civil War. After his wife divorced him, however, and his two sons died, he began to write to his friends of his premonition of his approaching death. Soon afterward, he vanished without a clue. His "An Occurrence at Owl Creek Bridge" is a favorite American masterpiece of his supernatural works. It offers a shocking twist at the end.

$\mathcal{A}$ man stood upon a railroad bridge in northern Alabama, looking down into the swift water twenty feet below. The man's hands were behind his back, the wrists bound with a cord. A rope closely encircled his neck. It was attached to a stout cross-timber above his head and the slack fell to the level of his knees. Some loose boards laid upon the sleepers supporting the metals of the railway supplied a footing for him and his executioners—two private soldiers of the Federal army, directed by a sergeant who in civil life may have been a deputy sheriff. At a short remove upon the same temporary platform was an officer in the uniform of his rank, armed. He was a captain. A sentinel at each end of the bridge stood with his rifle in the position known as "support," that is to say, vertical in front of the left shoulder, the hammer resting on the forearm thrown straight across the chest—a formal and unnatural position, enforcing an erect carriage of the body. It did not appear to be the duty of these two men to know what was occurring at the center of the bridge; they merely blockaded the two ends of the foot planking that traversed it. Beyond one of the sentinels nobody was in sight; the railroad ran straight away into a forest for a hundred yards, then, curving, was lost to view. Doubtless there was an outpost farther along. The other bank of the stream was open ground—a gentle acclivity topped with a stockade of vertical tree trunks, loopholed for rifles, with a single embrasure through which protruded the muzzle of a brass cannon commanding the bridge. Midway of the slope between the bridge and fort were the spectators—a single company of infantry in line, at "parade rest," the butts of the rifles on the ground, the barrels inclining slightly backward against the right shoulder, the hands crossed upon the stock. A lieutenant stood at the right of the line, the point of his sword upon the ground, his left hand resting upon his right. Excepting the group of four at the center of the bridge, not a man moved. The company faced the bridge, staring stonily, motionless. The sentinels, facing the banks of the stream, might have been statues to adorn the bridge. The captain stood with folded arms, silent, observing the work of his subordinates, but making no sign. Death is a dignitary who when he comes announced is to be received with formal manifestations of respect, even by those most familiar with him. In the code of military etiquette silence and fixity are forms of deference.

The man who was engaged in being hanged was apparently about thirty-five years of age. He was a civilian, if one might judge from his habit, which was that of a planter. His features were good—a straight nose, firm mouth, broad forehead, from which his long, dark hair was combed straight back, falling behind his ears to the collar of his well-fitting frock coat. He wore a mustache and pointed beard, but no whiskers. His eyes were large and dark gray, and had a kindly expression which one would hardly have expected in one whose neck was in the hemp. Evidently this was no vulgar assassin. The liberal military code makes provision for hanging many kinds of persons, and gentlemen are not excluded.

The preparations being complete, the two private soldiers stepped aside and each drew away the plank upon which he had been standing. The sergeant turned to the captain, saluted and placed himself immediately behind that officer, who in turn moved apart one pace. These movements left the condemned man and the sergeant standing on the two ends of the same plank, which spanned three of the cross-ties of the bridge. The end upon which the civilian stood almost, but not quite, reached a fourth. This plank had been held in place by the weight of the captain; it was now held by that of the sergeant. At a signal from the former the latter would step aside, the plank would tilt and the condemned man go down between two ties. The arrangement commended itself to his judgment as simple and effective. His face had not been covered nor his eyes bandaged. He looked a moment at his "unsteadfast footing," then let his gaze wander to the swirling water of the stream racing madly beneath his feet. A piece of dancing driftwood caught his attention and his eyes followed it down the current. How slowly it appeared to move. What a sluggish stream!

He closed his eyes in order to fix his last thoughts upon his wife and children. The water, touched to gold by the early sun, the brooding mists under the banks at some distance down the stream, the fort, the soldiers, the piece of drift—all had distracted him. And now he became conscious of a new disturbance. Striking through the thought of his dear ones was a sound which he could neither ignore nor understand, a sharp, distinct, metallic percussion like the stroke of a blacksmith's hammer upon the anvil; it had the same ringing quality. He wondered what it was, and whether immeasurably distant or nearby—it seemed both. Its recurrence was regular, but as slow as the tolling of a death knell. He awaited each stroke with impatience and—he knew not why—apprehension. The intervals of silence grew progressively longer, the delays became maddening. With their greater infrequency the sounds increased in strength and sharpness. They hurt his ear like the thrust of a knife; he feared he would shriek. What he heard was the ticking of his watch.

He unclosed his eyes and saw again the water below him. "If I could free my hands," he thought, "I might throw off the noose and spring into the stream. By diving I could evade the bullets and, swimming vigorously, reach the bank, take to the woods and get away home. My home, thank God, is as yet outside their lines; my wife and little ones are still beyond the invader's farthest advance."

As these thoughts, which have here to be set down in words, were flashed into the doomed man's brain rather than evolved from it, the captain nodded to the sergeant. The sergeant stepped aside. . . .

III

As Peyton Farquhar fell straight downward through the bridge he lost consciousness and was as one already dead. From this state he was awakened—ages later, it seemed to him—by the pain of a sharp pressure upon his throat, followed by a sense of suffocation. Keen, poignant agonies seemed to shoot from his neck downward through every fiber of his body and limbs. These pains appeared to flash along well-defined lines of ramification and to beat with an inconceivably rapid periodicity. They seemed like streams of pulsating fire heating him to an intolerable temperature. As to his head, he was conscious of nothing but a feeling of fullness—of congestion. These sensations were unaccompanied by thought. The intellectual part of his nature was already effaced; he had power only to feel, and feeling was torment. He was conscious of motion. Encompassed in a luminous cloud, of which he was now merely the fiery heart, without material substance, he swung through unthinkable arcs of oscillation, like a vast pendulum. Then all at once, with terrible suddenness, the light about him shot upward with the noise of a loud splash; a frightful roaring was in his ears, and all was cold and dark. The power of thought was restored; he knew that the rope had broken and he had fallen into the stream. There was no additional strangulation; the noose about his neck was already suffocating him and kept the water from his lungs. To die of hanging at the bottom of a river!—the idea seemed to him ludicrous. He opened his eyes in the darkness and saw above him a gleam of light, but how distant, how inaccessible! He was still sinking, for the light became fainter and fainter until it was a mere glimmer. Then it began to grow and brighten, and he knew that he was rising toward the surface— knew it with reluctance, for he was now very comfortable. "To be hanged and drowned," he thought, "that is not so bad; but I do not wish to be shot. No. I will not be shot. That is not fair."

He was not conscious of an effort, but a sharp pain in his wrist apprised him that he was trying to free his hands. He gave the struggle his attention, as an idler might observe the feat of a juggler, without interest in the outcome. What splendid effort!—what magnificent, what superhuman strength! Ah, that was a fine endeavor! Bravo! The cord fell away; his arms parted and floated upward, the hands dimly seen on each side in the growing light.

He watched them with a new interest as first one and then the other pounced upon the noose at his neck. They tore it away and thrust it fiercely aside, its undulations resembling those of a water snake. "Put it back, put it back!" He thought he shouted these words to his hands, for the undoing of the noose had been succeeded by the direst pang that he had yet experienced. His neck ached horribly; his brain was on fire; his heart, which had been fluttering faintly, gave a great leap, trying to force itself out at his mouth. His whole body was racked and wrenched with an insupportable anguish! But his disobedient hands gave no heed to the command. They beat the water vigorously with quick, downward strokes, forcing him to the surface. He felt his head emerge; his eyes were blinded by the sunlight; his chest expanded convulsively, and with a supreme and crowning agony his lungs engulfed a great draft of air, which instantly he expelled in a shriek!

He was now in full possession of his physical senses. They were, indeed, preternaturally keen and alert. Something in the awful disturbance of his organic system had so exalted and refined them that they made record of things never before perceived. He felt the ripples upon his face and heard their separate sounds as they struck. He looked at the forest on the bank of the stream, saw the individual trees, the leaves and the veining of each leaf—saw the very insects upon them: the locusts, the brilliant-bodied flies, the grey spiders stretching their webs from twig to twig. He noted the prismatic colors in all the dewdrops upon a million blades of grass. The humming of the gnats that danced above the eddies of the stream, the beating of the dragonflies' wings, the strokes of the water-spiders' legs, like oars which had lifted their boat—

all these made audible music. A fish slid along beneath his eyes and he heard the rush of its body parting the water.

He had come to the surface facing down the stream; in a moment the visible world seemed to wheel slowly round, himself the pivotal point, and he saw the bridge, the fort, the soldiers upon the bridge, the captain, the sergeant, the two privates, his executioners. They were in silhouette against the blue sky. They shouted and gesticulated, pointing at him. The captain had drawn his pistol, but did not fire; the others were unarmed. Their movements were grotesque and horrible, their forms gigantic.

Suddenly he heard a sharp report and something struck the water smartly within a few inches of his head, spattering his face with spray. He heard a second report, and saw one of the sentinels with his rifle at his shoulder, a light cloud of blue smoke rising from the muzzle. The man in the water saw the eye of the man on the bridge gazing into his own through the sights of the rifle. He observed that it was a grey eye and remembered having read that grey eyes were keenest, and that all famous marksmen had them. Nevertheless, this one had missed.

A counterswirl had caught Farquhar and turned him half round; he was again looking into the forest on the bank opposite the fort. The sound of a clear, high voice in a monotonous singsong now rang out behind him and came across the water with a distinctness that pierced and subdued all other sounds, even the beating of the ripples in his ears. Although no soldier, he had frequented camps enough to know the dread significance of that deliberate, drawling, aspirated chant; the lieutenant on shore was taking a part in the morning's work. How coldly and pitilessly—with what an even, calm intonation, presaging, and enforcing tranquillity in the men—with what accurately measured intervals fell those cruel words:

"Attention, company! . . . Shoulder arms! . . . Ready! . . . Aim! . . . Fire!"

Farquhar dived—dived as deeply as he could. The water roared in his ears like the voice of Niagara, yet he heard the dulled thunder of the volley and, rising again toward the surface, met shining bits of metal, singularly flattened, oscillating slowly downward. Some of them touched him on the face and hands, then fell away, continuing their descent. One lodged between his collar and neck; it was uncomfortably warm and he snatched it out.

As he rose to the surface, gasping for breath, he saw that he had been a long time under water; he was perceptibly farther downstream nearer to safety. The soldiers had almost finished reloading. The metal ramrods flashed all at once in the sunshine as they were drawn from the barrels, turned in the air, and thrust into their sockets. The two sentinels fired again, independently and ineffectually.

The hunted man saw all this over his shoulder; he was now swimming vigorously with the current. His brain was as energetic as his arms and legs; he thought with the rapidity of lightning.

"The officer," he reasoned, "will not make that martinet's error a second time. It is as easy to dodge a volley as a single shot. He has probably already given the command to fire at will. God help me, I cannot dodge them all!"

An appalling plash within two yards of him was followed by a loud, rushing sound, diminuendo, which seemed to travel back through the air to the fort and died in an explosion which stirred the very river to its deeps!

A rising sheet of water curved over him, fell down upon him, blinded him, strangled him! The cannon had taken a hand in the game. As he shook his head free from the commotion of the smitten water he heard the deflected shot humming through the air ahead, and in an instant it was cracking and smashing the branches in the forest beyond.

"They will not do that again," he thought; "the next time they will use a charge of grape. I must keep my eye upon the gun. The smoke will apprise me—the report arrives too late; it lags behind the missile. That is a good gun."

Suddenly he felt himself whirled round and round—spinning like a top. The water, the banks, the forests, the now distant bridge, fort and men—all were commingled and blurred. Objects were represented by their colors only; circular horizontal streaks of color—that was all he saw. He had been caught in a vortex and was being whirled on with a velocity of advance and gyration that made him giddy and sick. In a few moments he was flung upon the gravel at the foot of the left bank of the stream—the southern bank—and behind a projecting point which concealed him from his enemies. The sudden arrest of his motion, the abrasion of one of his hands on the gravel, restored him, and he wept with delight. He dug his fingers into the sand, threw it over himself in handfuls and audibly blessed it. It looked like diamonds, rubies, emeralds; he could think of nothing beautiful which it did not resemble. The trees upon the bank were giant garden plants; he noted a definite order in their arrangement, inhaled the fragrance of their blooms. A strange, roseate light shone through the spaces among their trunks and the wind made in their branches the music of Æolian harps. He had no wish to perfect his escape—was content to remain in that enchanting spot until retaken.

A whiz and rattle of grapeshot among the branches high above his head roused him from his dream. The baffled cannoneer had fired him a random farewell. He sprang to his feet, rushed up the sloping bank, and plunged into the forest.

All that day he traveled, laying his course by the rounding sun. The forest seemed interminable; nowhere did he discover a break in it, not even a woodman's road. He had not known that he lived in so wild a region. There was something uncanny in the revelation.

By nightfall he was fatigued, footsore, famished. The thought of his wife and children urged him on. At last he found a road which led him in what he knew to be the right direction. It was as wide and straight as a city street, yet it seemed untraveled. No fields bordered it, no dwelling anywhere. Not so much as the barking of a dog suggested human habitation. The black bodies of the trees formed a straight wall on both sides, terminating on the horizon in a point, like a diagram in a lesson in perspective. Overhead, as he looked up through this rift in the wood, shone great garden stars looking unfamiliar and grouped in strange constellations. He was sure they were arranged in some order which had a secret and malign significance. The wood on either side was full of singular noises, among which—once, twice, and again—he distinctly heard whispers in an unknown tongue.

His neck was in pain and lifting his hand to it found it horribly swollen. He knew that it had a circle of black where the rope had bruised it. His eyes felt congested; he could no longer close them. His tongue was swollen with thirst; he relieved its fever by thrusting it forward from between his teeth into the cold air. How softly the turf had carpeted the untraveled avenue—he could no longer feel the roadway beneath his feet!

Doubtless, despite his suffering, he had fallen asleep while walking, for now he sees another scene—perhaps he has merely recovered from a delirium. He stands at the gate of his own home. All is as he left it, and all bright and beautiful in the morning sunshine. He must have traveled the entire night. As he pushes open the gate and passes up the wide white walk, he sees a flutter of female garments; his wife, looking fresh and cool and sweet, steps down from the veranda to meet him. At the bottom of the steps she stands waiting, with a smile of ineffable joy, an attitude of matchless grace and dignity. Ah, how beautiful she is! He springs forward with extended arms. As he is about to clasp her he feels a stunning blow upon the back of the neck; a blinding white light blazes all about him with a sound like the shock of a cannon—then all is darkness and silence!

Peyton Farquhar was dead; his body, with a broken neck, swung gently from side to side beneath the timbers of the Owl Creek bridge.

The Dead Girl

Guy de Maupassant
(1850–1893)

Born in France to minor aristocrats, Guy de Maupassant was a skillful literary master whose professional reputation and success belie his personal agony. By the age of twenty, he knew he was afflicted with the maddening disease of syphilis, and his sanity gradually began to slip away. Nevertheless, he enjoyed an active life, perhaps in part because he rejected the day's standard treatment of ingesting mercury. The author loved to travel, and he spent much time aboard his little yacht journeying over the seas. It would be simple to conclude that he was just an adventurer, but in just one decade, between 1880 and 1890, Maupassant accomplished a grand lifetime of literary achievement. The prolific writer published three hundred short stories, six novels, three travel books, and a volume of verse. His stories were translated all over the world. It was in his work where he permitted himself to explore the cross he would bear: the horrific realities of going mad and preparing for an imminent death. Eventually, his life and career did succumb to his madness, and in 1892, he tried to put an end to his personal torture by slitting his throat. He was committed to an asylum, where he died a year later at the age of forty-two. Today, Maupassant's reputation is but a shadow of the man he was. Only a small handful of his works is readily published. "The Dead Girl," which was also translated under the title "Was It a Dream?," is one of his most famous and explores the nature of truth. It's a seemingly simple story, but make no bones about it: It's Maupassant's literary genius that takes such a rumpled theme and smooths it out over a few thin pages, making it quite useful.

I had loved her madly!

Why does one love? Why does one love? How queer it is to see only one being in the world, to have only one thought in one's mind, only one desire in the heart, and only one name on the lips—a name which comes up continually, rising, like the water in a spring, from the depths of the soul to the lips, a name which one repeats over and over again, which one whispers ceaselessly, everywhere, like a prayer.

I am going to tell you our story, for love only has one, which is always the same. I met her and loved her; that is all. And for a whole year I have lived on her tenderness, on her caresses, in her arms, in her dresses, on her words, so completely wrapped up, bound, and absorbed in everything which came up from her, that I no longer cared whether it was day or night, or whether I was dead or alive on this old earth of ours.

And then she died. How? I do not know; I no longer know anything. But one evening she came home wet, for it was raining heavily, and the next day she coughed, and she coughed for about a week, and took to her bed. What happened I do not remember now, but the doctors came, wrote, and went away. Medicines were brought, and some women made her drink them. Her hands were hot, her forehead was burning, and her eyes bright and sad. When I spoke to her, she answered me, but I do not remember what we said. I have forgotten everything, everything, everything! She died, and I very well remember her slight, feeble sigh. The nurse said: "Ah!" and I understood, I understood!

I knew nothing more, nothing. I saw a priest, who said: "Your mistress?" and it seemed to me as if he were insulting her. As she was dead, nobody had the right to say that any longer, and I turned him out. Another came who was very kind and tender, and I shed tears when he spoke to me about her.

They consulted me about the funeral, but I do not remember anything that they said, though I recollected the coffin, and the sound of the hammer when they nailed her down in it. Oh! God, God!

She was buried! Buried! She! In that hole! Some people came—female friends. I made my escape and ran away. I ran, and then walked through the streets, went home, and the next day started on a journey.

Yesterday I returned to Paris, and when I saw my room again—our room, our bed, our furniture, everything that remains of the life of a human being after death—I was seized by such a violent attack of fresh grief that I felt like opening the window and throwing myself out into the street. I could not remain any longer among these things, between these walls which had enclosed and sheltered her, which retained a thousand atoms of her, of her skin and of her breath, in their imperceptible crevices. I took up my hat to make my escape, and just as I reached the door, I passed the large glass in the hall, which she had put there so that she might look at herself every day from head to foot as she went out, to see if her toilette looked well, and was correct and pretty, from her little boots to her bonnet.

I stopped short in front of that looking-glass in which she had so often been reflected—so often, so often that it must have retained her reflection. I was standing there, trembling, with my eyes fixed on the glass—on that flat, profound, empty glass—which had contained her entirely, and had possessed her as much as I, as my passionate looks had. I felt as if I loved that glass. I touched it; it was cold. Oh! The recollection! Sorrowful mirror, burning mirror, horrible mirror, to make men suffer such torments! Happy is the man whose heart forgets everything that it has contained, everything that has passed before it, everything that has looked at itself in it, or has been reflected in its affection, its love! How I suffer!

I went out without knowing it, without wishing it, and toward the cemetery. I found her simple grave, a white marble cross, with these few words:

She loved, was loved, and died.

She is there, below, decayed! How horrible! I sobbed with my forehead on the ground, and I stopped there for a long time, a long time. Then I saw that it was getting dark, and a strange, mad wish, the wish of a despairing lover, seized me. I wished to pass the night, the last night, in weeping on her grave. But I should be seen and driven out. How was I to manage? I was cunning, and got up and began to roam about in that city of the dead. I walked and walked. How small this city is, in comparison with the other, the city in which we live. And yet, how much more numerous the dead are than the living. We want high houses, wide streets, and much room for the four generations who see the daylight at the same time, drink water from the spring, and wine from the vines, and eat bread from the plains.

And for all the generations of the dead, for all that ladder of humanity that has descended down to us, there is scarcely anything, scarcely anything! The earth takes them back, and oblivion effaces them. Adieu!

At the end of the cemetery, I suddenly perceived that I was in the oldest part, where those who had been dead a long time are mingling with the soil, where the crosses themselves are decayed, where possibly newcomers will be put tomorrow. It is full of untended roses, of strong and dark cypress trees, a sad and beautiful garden, nourished on human flesh.

I was alone, perfectly alone. So I crouched in a green tree and hid myself there completely amid the thick and somber branches. I waited, clinging to the stem, like a shipwrecked man does to a plank.

When it was quite dark, I left my refuge and began to walk softly, slowly, inaudibly, through that ground full of dead people. I wandered about for a long time, but could not find her tomb again. I went on with extended arms, knocking against the tombs with my hands, my feet, my knees, my chest, even with my head, without being able to find her. I groped about like a blind man finding his way, I felt the stones, the crosses, the iron railings, the metal wreaths, and the wreaths of faded flowers! I read the names with my fingers, by passing them over the letters. What a night! What a night! I could not find her again!

There was no other moon. What a night! I was fright-

ened, horribly frightened in these narrow paths, between
two rows of graves. Graves! Graves! Graves! Nothing but
graves! On my right, on my left, in front of me, around
me, everywhere there were graves! I sat down on one of
them, for I could not walk any longer, my knees were so
weak. I could hear my heart beat! And I heard something
else as well. What? A confused, nameless noise. Was the
noise in my head, in the impenetrable night, or beneath
the mysterious earth, the earth sown with human corpses?
I looked all around me, but I cannot say how long I remained there; I was paralyzed with terror, cold with fright,
ready to shout out, ready to die.

Suddenly, it seemed to me that the slab of marble on
which I was sitting, was moving. Certainly it was moving,
as if it were being raised. With a bound, I sprang onto the
neighboring tomb, and I saw, yes, I distinctly saw the
stone which I had just quitted rise upright. Then the dead
person appeared, a naked skeleton, pushing the stone
back with its bent back. I saw it quite clearly, although
the night was so dark. On the cross I could read:

*Here lies Jacques Olivant, who died at the age of fifty-
one. He loved his family, was kind and honorable,
and died in the grace of the Lord.*

The dead man also read what was inscribed on his
tombstone; then he picked up a stone off the path, a
little, pointed stone, and began to scrape the letters
carefully. He slowly effaced them, and with the hollows
of his eyes he looked at the places where they had
been engraved. Then with the tip of the bone that had
been his forefinger, he wrote in luminous letters, like

those lines which boys trace on walls with the tip of a lucifer match:

> *Here reposes Jacques Olivant, who died at the age of fifty-one. He hastened his father's death by his unkindness, as he wished to inherit his fortune; he tortured his wife, tormented his children, deceived his neighbors, robbed everyone he could, and died wretched.*

When he had finished writing, the dead man stood motionless, looking at his work. On turning round I saw that all the graves were open, that all the dead bodies had emerged from them, and that all had effaced the lies inscribed on the gravestones by their relations, substituting the truth instead. And I saw that all had been the tormentors of their neighbors—malicious, dishonest, hypocrites, liars, rogues, calumniators, envious; that they had stolen, deceived, performed every disgraceful, every abominable action, these good fathers, these faithful wives, these devoted sons, these chaste daughters, these honest tradesmen, these men and women who were called irreproachable. They were all writing at the same time, on the threshold of their eternal abode, the truth, the terrible and the holy truth of which everybody was ignorant, or pretended to be ignorant, while they were alive.

I thought that *she* also must have written something on her tombstone, and now running without any fear among the half-open coffins, among the corpses and the skeletons, I went toward her, sure that I should find her immediately. I recognized her at once, without seeing her face, which was covered by the winding-sheet, and on the marble cross, where shortly before I had read:

She loved, was loved, and died.

I now saw:

Having gone out in the rain one day, in order to deceive her lover, she caught cold and died.

It appears that they found me at daybreak, lying on the grave unconscious.

The Story of the Inexperienced Ghost

H. G. Wells
(1866–1946)

Utter the name H. G. Wells and *The War of the Worlds*, *The Time Machine*, and *The Invisible Man* quickly come to mind. Herbert George Wells was born in Bromley in Kent, England, the son of a shopkeeper and lady's maid. During his years as a student he studied biology, but was drawn to writing, and upon his graduation, he combined teaching with scientific journalism. Just a few years later, he envisioned a unique genre: science fiction. In 1895, *The Time Machine* was published and he made a place for himself in literary history. At the same time, he explored another realm of fiction: the life of the ordinary man. For the next fifteen years, he developed these themes side by side and was remarkably productive. In his later years, he moved to themes that were more scientific and social in focus, such as *The Science of Life* and *The Fate of Homo Sapiens*, but by the Second World War, his hopes for mankind were giving way to despair. Over the years, he had speculated with great conviction that science would raise man above himself and make life better, but now he believed the opposite was coming to pass. He saw a world that was anything but the sane, free world he dreamed of. His last book, published in 1945, was appropriately titled *Mind at the End of Its Tether*. "The Story of the Inexperienced Ghost" comes from his collection *Twelve Stories and a Dream*, published in 1903. A joy to read, it's a look at what one man might conjure up for sport, and what another might believe. It's up to you to decide who's who in this riddle of a story.

*T*he scene amidst which Clayton told his last story comes back very vividly to my mind. There he sat, for the greater part of the time, in the corner of the authentic settle by the spacious open fire, and Sanderson sat beside him smoking the Broseley clay that bore his name. There was Evans, and that marvel among actors, Wish, who is also a modest man. We had all come down to the Mermaid Club that Saturday morning, except Clayton, who had slept there overnight—which indeed gave him the opening of his story. We had golfed until golfing was invisible; we had dined, and we were in that mood of tranquil kindliness when men will suffer a story. When Clayton began to tell one, we naturally supposed he was lying. It may be that indeed he was lying—of that the reader will speedily be able to judge as well as I. He began, it is true, with an air of matter-of-fact anecdote, but that we thought was only the incurable artifice of the man.

"I say!" he remarked, after a long consideration of the upward rain of sparks from the log that Sanderson had thumped. "You know I was alone here last night?"

"Except for the domestics," said Wish.

"Who sleep in the other wing," said Clayton. "Yes. Well—" He pulled at his cigar for some little time as though he still hesitated about his confidence. Then he said, quite quietly, "I caught a ghost!"

"Caught a ghost, did you?" said Sanderson. "Where is it?"

And Evans, who admires Clayton immensely and has been four weeks in America, shouted, "CAUGHT a ghost, did you, Clayton? I'm glad of it! Tell us all about it right now."

Clayton said he would in a minute, and asked him to shut the door.

He looked apologetically at me. "There's no eavesdropping of course, but we don't want to upset our very excellent service with any rumors of ghosts in the place. There's too much shadow and oak paneling to trifle with that. And this, you know, wasn't a regular ghost. I don't think it will come again—ever."

"You mean to say you didn't keep it?" said Sanderson.

"I hadn't the heart to," said Clayton.

And Sanderson said he was surprised.

We laughed, and Clayton looked aggrieved. "I know," he said, with the flicker of a smile, "but the fact is it really WAS a ghost, and I'm as sure of it as I am that I am talking to you now. I'm not joking. I mean what I say."

Sanderson drew deeply at his pipe, with one reddish eye on Clayton, and then emitted a thin jet of smoke more eloquent than many words. Clayton ignored the comment. "It is the strangest thing that has ever happened in my life. You know, I never believed in ghosts or anything of the sort, before, ever; and then, you know, I bag one in a corner; and the whole business is in my hands."

He meditated still more profoundly, and produced

and began to pierce a second cigar with a curious little stabber he affected.

"You talked to it?" asked Wish.

"For the space, probably, of an hour."

"Chatty?" I said, joining the party of the skeptics.

"The poor devil was in trouble," said Clayton, bowed over his cigar-end and with the very faintest note of reproof.

"Sobbing?" someone asked.

Clayton heaved a realistic sigh at the memory. "Good Lord!" he said. "Yes." And then, "Poor fellow! Yes."

"Where did you strike it?" asked Evans, in his best American accent.

"I never realized," said Clayton, ignoring him, "the poor sort of thing a ghost might be," and he hung us up again for a time while he sought for matches in his pocket and lit and warmed to his cigar.

"I took an advantage," he reflected at last.

We were none of us in a hurry. "A character," he said, "remains just the same character for all that it's been disembodied. That's a thing we too often forget. People with a certain strength or fixity of purpose may have ghosts of a certain strength and fixity of purpose—most haunting ghosts, you know, must be as one-idea'd as monomaniacs and as obstinate as mules to come back again and again. This poor creature wasn't." He suddenly looked up rather queerly, and his eye went round the room. "I say it," he said, "in all kindliness, but that is the plain truth of the case. Even at the first glance he struck me as weak."

He punctuated with the help of his cigar.

"I came upon him, you know, in the long passage. His back was towards me and I saw him first. Right off I knew him for a ghost. He was transparent and whitish; clean through his chest I could see the glimmer of the little window at the end. And not only his physique but his attitude struck me as being weak. He looked, you know, as though he didn't know in the slightest whatever he meant to do. One hand was on the paneling and the other fluttered to his mouth. Like—SO!"

"What sort of physique?" said Sanderson.

"Lean. You know that sort of young man's neck that has two great flutings down the back, here and here—so! And a little, meanish head with scrubby hair—and rather bad ears. Shoulders bad, narrower than the hips; turn-down collar, ready-made short jacket, trousers baggy and a little frayed at the heels. That's how he took me. I came very quietly up the staircase. I did not carry a light, you know—the candles are on the landing table and there is that lamp—and I was in my list slippers, and I saw him as I came up. I stopped dead at that—taking him in. I wasn't a bit afraid. I think that in most of these affairs one is never nearly so afraid or excited as one imagines one would be. I was surprised and interested. I thought, 'Good Lord! Here's a ghost at last! And I haven't believed for a moment in ghosts during the last five-and-twenty years.' "

"Um," said Wish.

"I suppose I wasn't on the landing a moment before he found out I was there. He turned on me sharply, and I saw the face of an immature young man, a weak nose, a scrubby little mustache, a feeble chin. So for an instant we stood—he looking over his shoulder at me—and re-garded one another. Then he seemed to remember his high calling. He turned round, drew himself up, projected his face, raised his arms, spread his hands in approved ghost fashion—came towards me. As he did so his little jaw dropped, and he emitted a faint, drawn-out 'Boo.' No, it wasn't—not a bit dreadful. I'd dined. I'd had a bottle of champagne, and being all alone, perhaps two or three—perhaps even four or five—whiskies, so I was as solid as rocks and no more frightened than if I'd been assailed by a frog. 'Boo!' I said. 'Nonsense. You don't belong to THIS place. What are you doing here?'

"I could see him wince. 'Boo-oo,' he said.

" 'Boo—be hanged! Are you a member?' I said; and just to show I didn't care a pin for him I stepped through a corner of him and made to light my candle. 'Are you a member?' I repeated, looking at him sideways.

"He moved a little so as to stand clear of me, and his bearing became crestfallen. 'No,' he said, in answer to the persistent interrogation of my eye; 'I'm not a member—I'm a ghost.'

" 'Well, that doesn't give you the run of the Mermaid Club. Is there anyone you want to see, or anything of that sort?' and doing it as steadily as possible for fear that he should mistake the carelessness of whisky for the distraction of fear, I got my candle alight. I turned on him, holding it. 'What are you doing here?' I said.

"He had dropped his hands and stopped his booing, and there he stood, abashed and awkward, the ghost of a weak, silly, aimless young man. 'I'm haunting,' he said.

" 'You haven't any business to,' I said in a quiet voice.

" 'I'm a ghost,' he said, as if in defense.

" 'That may be, but you haven't any business to haunt here. This is a respectable private club; people often stop here with nursemaids and children, and, going about in the careless way you do, some poor little mite could easily come upon you and be scared out of her wits. I suppose you didn't think of that?'

" 'No, sir,' he said, 'I didn't.'

" 'You should have done. You haven't any claim on the place, have you? Weren't murdered here, or anything of that sort?'

" 'None, sir; but I thought as it was old and oak-paneled—'

" 'That's NO excuse.' I regarded him firmly. 'Your coming here is a mistake,' I said, in a tone of friendly superiority. I feigned to see if I had my matches, and then looked up at him frankly. 'If I were you I wouldn't wait for cock-crow—I'd vanish right away.'

"He looked embarrassed. 'The fact IS, sir—' he began.

" 'I'd vanish,' I said, driving it home.

" 'The fact is, sir, that—somehow—I can't.'

" 'You CAN'T?'

" 'No, sir. There's something I've forgotten. I've been hanging about here since midnight last night, hiding in the cupboards of the empty bedrooms and things like that. I'm flurried. I've never come haunting before, and it seems to put me out.'

" 'Put you out?'

" 'Yes, sir. I've tried to do it several times, and it doesn't come off. There's some little thing has slipped me, and I can't get back.'

"That, you know, rather bowled me over. He looked at me in such an abject way that for the life of me I couldn't keep up quite the high, hectoring vein I had adopted. 'That's queer,' I said, and as I spoke I fancied I heard someone moving about down below. 'Come into my room and tell me more about it,' I said. 'I didn't, of course, understand this,' and I tried to take him by the arm. But, of course, you might as well have tried to take hold of a puff of smoke! I had forgotten my number, I think. Anyhow, I remember going into several bedrooms—it was lucky I was the only soul in that wing—until I saw my traps. 'Here we are,' I said, and sat down in the armchair; 'sit down and tell me all about it. It seems to me you have got yourself into a jolly awkward position, old chap.'

"Well, he said he wouldn't sit down! He'd prefer to flit up and down the room if it was all the same to me. And so he did, and in a little while we were deep in a long and serious talk. And presently, you know, something of those whiskies and sodas evaporated out of me, and I began to realize just a little what a thundering rum and weird business it was that I was in. There he was, semi-transparent—the proper conventional phantom, and noiseless except for his ghost of a voice—flitting to and fro in that nice, clean, chintz-hung old bedroom. You could see the gleam of the copper candlesticks through him, and the lights on the brass fender, and the corners of the framed engravings on the wall, and there he was telling me all about this wretched little life of his that had recently ended on earth. He hadn't a particularly honest face, you know, but being transparent, of course, he couldn't avoid telling the truth."

"Eh?" said Wish, suddenly sitting up in his chair.

"What?" said Clayton.

"Being transparent—couldn't avoid telling the truth— I don't see it," said Wish.

"*I* don't see it," said Clayton, with inimitable assurance. "But it IS so, I can assure you nevertheless. I don't believe he got once a nail's breadth off the Bible truth. He told me how he had been killed—he went down into a London basement with a candle to look for a leakage of gas—and described himself as a senior English master in a London private school when that release occurred."

"Poor wretch!" said I.

"That's what I thought, and the more he talked the more I thought it. There he was, purposeless in life and purposeless out of it. He talked of his father and mother and his schoolmaster, and all who had ever been any-thing to him in the world, meanly. He had been too sen-sitive, too nervous; none of them had ever valued him properly or understood him, he said. He had never had a real friend in the world, I think; he had never had a suc-cess. He had shirked games and failed examinations. 'It's like that with some people,' he said; 'whenever I got into the examination room or anywhere everything seemed to go.' Engaged to be married of course—to another over-sensitive person, I suppose—when the indiscretion with the gas escape ended his affairs. 'And where are you now?' I asked. 'Not in—?'

"He wasn't clear on that point at all. The impression he gave me was of a sort of vague, intermediate state, a special reserve for souls too non-existent for anything so positive as either sin or virtue. *I* don't know. He was much too egotistical and unobservant to give me any clear idea of the kind of place, kind of country, there is on the Other Side of Things. Wherever he was, he seems to have fallen in with a set of kindred spirits: ghosts of weak Cockney young men, who were on a footing of Christian names, and among these there was certainly a lot of talk about 'going haunting' and things like that. Yes—going haunting! They seemed to think 'haunting' a tremendous adventure, and most of them funked it all the time. And so primed, you know, he had come."

"But really!" said Wish to the fire.

"These are the impressions he gave me, anyhow," said Clayton, modestly. "I may, of course, have been in a rather uncritical state, but that was the sort of background he gave to himself. He kept flitting up and down, with his thin voice going talking, talking about his wretched self, and never a word of clear, firm statement from first to last. He was thinner and sillier and more pointless than if he had been real and alive. Only then, you know, he would not have been in my bedroom here—if he HAD been alive. I should have kicked him out."

"Of course," said Evans, "there ARE poor mortals like that."

"And there's just as much chance of their having ghosts as the rest of us," I admitted.

"What gave a sort of point to him, you know, was the fact that he did seem within limits to have found himself out. The mess he had made of haunting had depressed him terribly. He had been told it would be a 'lark'; he had come expecting it to be a 'lark,' and here it was, nothing but another failure added to his record! He proclaimed himself an utter out-and-out failure. He said, and I can quite believe it, that he had never tried to do anything all his life that he hadn't made a perfect mess of—and through all the wastes of eternity he never would. If he had had sympathy, perhaps— He paused at that, and stood regarding me. He remarked that, strange as it might seem to me, nobody, not anyone, ever, had given him the amount of sympathy I was doing now. I could see what he wanted straightaway, and I determined to head him off at once. I may be a brute, you know, but being the Only Real Friend, the recipient of the confidences of one of these egotistical weaklings, ghost or body, is beyond my physical endurance. I got up briskly. 'Don't you brood on these things too much,' I said. 'The thing you've got to do is to get out of this, get out of this—sharp. You pull yourself together and TRY.' 'I can't,' he said. 'You try,' I said, and try he did."

"Try!" said Sanderson. "HOW?"

"Passes," said Clayton.

"Passes?"

"Complicated series of gestures and passes with the hands. That's how he had come in and that's how he had to get out again. Lord! What a business I had!"

"But how could ANY series of passes—?" I began.

"My dear man," said Clayton, turning on me and putting a great emphasis on certain words, "you want EVERYTHING clear. *I* don't know HOW. All I know is that you DO—that HE did, anyhow, at least. After a fearful time, you know, he got his passes right and suddenly disappeared."

"Did you," said Sanderson, slowly, "observe the passes?"

"Yes," said Clayton, and seemed to think. "It was tremendously queer," he said. "There we were, I and this thin vague ghost, in that silent room, in this silent, empty inn, in this silent little Friday-night town. Not a sound except our voices and a faint panting he made when he swung. There was the bedroom candle, and one candle on the dressing table alight, that was all—sometimes one or other would flare up into a tall, lean, astonished flame for a space. And queer things happened. 'I can't,' he said; 'I shall never—!' And suddenly he sat down on a little chair at the foot of the bed and began to sob and sob. Lord! What a harrowing, whimpering thing he seemed!

" 'You pull yourself together,' I said, and tried to pat

him on the back, and . . . my confounded hand went through him! By that time, you know, I wasn't nearly so—massive as I had been on the landing. I got the queerness of it full. I remember snatching back my hand out of him, as it were, with a little thrill, and walking over to the dressing table. 'You pull yourself together,' I said to him, 'and try.' And in order to encourage and help him I began to try as well."

"What!" said Sanderson. "The passes?"

"Yes, the passes."

"But—" I said, moved by an idea that eluded me for a space.

"This is interesting," said Sanderson, with his finger in his pipe-bowl. "You mean to say this ghost of yours gave away—"

"Did his level best to give away the whole confounded barrier? YES."

"He didn't," said Wish; "he couldn't. Or you'd have gone there too."

"That's precisely it," I said, finding my elusive idea put into words for me.

"That IS precisely it," said Clayton, with thoughtful eyes upon the fire.

For just a little while there was silence.

"And at last he did it?" said Sanderson.

"At last he did it. I had to keep him up to it hard, but he did it at last—rather suddenly. He despaired, we had a scene, and then he got up abruptly and asked me to go through the whole performance, slowly, so that he might see. 'I believe,' he said, 'if I could SEE I should spot what was wrong at once.' And he did. '*I* know,' he said. 'What do you know?' said I. '*I* know,' he repeated. Then he said, peevishly, 'I CAN'T do it if you look at me—I really

CAN'T; it's been that, partly, all along. I'm such a nervous fellow that you put me out.' Well, we had a bit of an argument. Naturally I wanted to see; but he was as obstinate as a mule, and suddenly I had come over as tired as a dog—he tired me out. 'All right,' I said, '*I* won't look at you,' and turned towards the mirror, on the wardrobe, by the bed.

"He started off very fast. I tried to follow him by looking in the looking glass, to see just what it was had hung. Round went his arms and his hands, so, and so, and so, and then with a rush came to the last gesture of all—you stand erect and open out your arms—and so, don't you know, he stood. And then he didn't! He didn't! He wasn't! I wheeled round from the looking glass to him. There was nothing! I was alone, with the flaring candles and a staggering mind. What had happened? Had anything happened? Had I been dreaming? . . . And then, with an absurd note of finality about it, the clock upon the landing discovered the moment was ripe for striking ONE. So!— Ping! And I was as grave and sober as a judge, with all my champagne and whisky gone into the vast serene. Feeling queer, you know—confoundedly QUEER! Queer! Good Lord!"

He regarded his cigar-ash for a moment. "That's all that happened," he said.

"And then you went to bed?" asked Evans.

"What else was there to do?"

I looked Wish in the eye. We wanted to scoff, and there was something, something perhaps in Clayton's voice and manner, that hampered our desire.

"And about these passes?" said Sanderson.

"I believe I could do them now."

"Oh!" said Sanderson, and produced a penknife and set himself to grub the dottel out of the bowl of his clay.

"Why don't you do them now?" said Sanderson, shutting his penknife with a click.

"That's what I'm going to do," said Clayton.

"They won't work," said Evans.

"If they do—" I suggested.

"You know, I'd rather you didn't," said Wish, stretching out his legs.

"Why?" asked Evans.

"I'd rather he didn't," said Wish.

"But he hasn't got 'em right," said Sanderson, plugging too much tobacco in his pipe.

"All the same, I'd rather he didn't," said Wish.

We argued with Wish. He said that for Clayton to go through those gestures was like mocking a serious matter. "But you don't believe—?" I said. Wish glanced at Clayton, who was staring into the fire, weighing something in his mind. "I do—more than half, anyhow, I do," said Wish.

"Clayton," said I, "you're too good a liar for us. Most of it was all right. But that disappearance . . . happened to be convincing. Tell us, it's a tale of cock and bull."

He stood up without heeding me, took the middle of the hearth rug, and faced me. For a moment he regarded his feet thoughtfully, and then for all the rest of the time his eyes were on the opposite wall, with an intent expression. He raised his two hands slowly to the level of his eyes and so began. . . .

Now, Sanderson is a Freemason, a member of the lodge of the Four Kings, which devotes itself so ably to the study and elucidation of all the mysteries of Masonry past and present, and among the students of this lodge

Sanderson is by no means the least. He followed Clayton's motions with a singular interest in his reddish eye. "That's not bad," he said, when it was done. "You really do, you know, put things together, Clayton, in a most amazing fashion. But there's one little detail out."

"I know," said Clayton. "I believe I could tell you which."

"Well?"

"This," said Clayton, and did a queer little twist and writhing and thrust of the hands.

"Yes."

"That, you know, was what HE couldn't get right," said Clayton. "But how do YOU—?"

"Most of this business, and particularly how you invented it, I don't understand at all," said Sanderson, "but just that phase—I do." He reflected. "These happen to be a series of gestures—connected with a certain branch of esoteric Masonry. Probably you know. Or else—HOW?" He reflected still further. "I do not see I can do any harm in telling you just the proper twist. After all, if you know, you know; if you don't, you don't."

"I know nothing," said Clayton, "except what the poor devil let out last night."

"Well, anyhow," said Sanderson, and placed his churchwarden very carefully upon the shelf over the fireplace. Then very rapidly he gesticulated with his hands.

"So?" said Clayton, repeating.

"So," said Sanderson, and took his pipe in hand again.

"Ah, NOW," said Clayton, "I can do the whole thing—right."

He stood up before the waning fire and smiled at us

all. But I think there was just a little hesitation in his smile. "If I begin—" he said.

"I wouldn't begin," said Wish.

"It's all right!" said Evans. "Matter is indestructible. You don't think any jiggery-pokery of this sort is going to snatch Clayton into the world of shades. Not it! You may try, Clayton, so far as I'm concerned, until your arms drop off at the wrists."

"I don't believe that," said Wish, and stood up and put his arm on Clayton's shoulder. "You've made me half believe in that story somehow, and I don't want to see the thing done!"

"Goodness!" said I. "Here's Wish frightened!"

"I am," said Wish, with real or admirably feigned intensity. "I believe that if he goes through these motions right he'll GO."

"He'll not do anything of the sort," I cried. "There's only one way out of this world for men, and Clayton is thirty years from that. Besides . . . And such a ghost! Do you think—?"

Wish interrupted me by moving. He walked out from among our chairs and stopped beside the tole and stood there. "Clayton," he said, "you're a fool."

Clayton, with a humorous light in his eyes, smiled back at him. "Wish," he said, "is right and all you others are wrong. I shall go. I shall get to the end of these passes, and as the last swish whistles through the air, Presto!—this hearth rug will be vacant, the room will be blank amazement, and a respectably dressed gentleman of fifteen stone will plump into the world of shades. I'm certain. So will you be. I decline to argue further. Let the thing be tried."

"NO," said Wish, and made a step and ceased, and Clayton raised his hands once more to repeat the spirit's passing.

By that time, you know, we were all in a state of tension—largely because of the behavior of Wish. We sat all of us with our eyes on Clayton—I, at least, with a sort of tight, stiff feeling about me as though from the back of my skull to the middle of my thighs my body had been changed to steel. And there, with a gravity that was imperturbably serene, Clayton bowed and swayed and waved his hands and arms before us. As he drew towards the end one piled up, one tingled in one's teeth. The last gesture, I have said, was to swing the arms out wide open, with the face held up. And when at last he swung out to this closing gesture I ceased even to breathe. It was ridiculous, of course, but you know that ghost-story feeling. It was after dinner, in a queer, old shadowy house. Would he, after all—?

There he stood for one stupendous moment, with his arms open and his upturned face, assured and bright, in the glare of the hanging lamp. We hung through that moment as if it were an age, and then came from all of us something that was half a sigh of infinite relief and half a reassuring "NO!" For visibly—he wasn't going. It was all nonsense. He had told an idle story, and carried it almost to conviction, that was all! . . . And then in that moment the face of Clayton changed.

It changed. It changed as a lit house changes when its lights are suddenly extinguished. His eyes were suddenly eyes that were fixed, his smile was frozen on his lips, and he stood there still. He stood there, very gently swaying.

That moment, too, was an age. And then, you know,

chairs were scraping, things were falling, and we were all
moving. His knees seemed to give, and he fell forward,
and Evans rose and caught him in his arms. . . .

It stunned us all. For a minute I suppose no one said
a coherent thing. We believed it, yet could not believe
it. . . . I came out of a muddled stupefaction to find myself kneeling beside him, and his vest and shirt were torn
open, and Sanderson's hand lay on his heart. . . .

Well—the simple fact before us could very well wait
our convenience; there was no hurry for us to compre-
hend. It lay there for an hour; it lies athwart my memory,
black and amazing still, to this day. Clayton had, indeed,
passed into the world that lies so near to and so far from
our own, and he had gone thither by the only road that
mortal man may take. But whether he did indeed pass
there by that poor ghost's incantation, or whether he was
stricken suddenly by apoplexy in the midst of an idle
tale—as the coroner's jury would have us believe—is no
matter for my judging; it is just one of those inexplicable
riddles that must remain unsolved until the final solution
of all things shall come. All I certainly know is that, in the
very moment, in the very instant, of concluding those
passes, he changed, and staggered, and fell down before
us—dead!

The Return

R. Murray Gilchrist
(1868–1917)

Critics say that the landscape came to life in Gilchrist's works, and his descriptive powers were formidable. Robert Murray Gilchrist was considered a master of the Victorian style of ghost story, yet he is forgotten today. In fact, any information about the man is scarce. Primarily a novelist of the late nineteenth century, he wrote only one collection of ghost and supernatural stories, *The Stone Dragon*. A rare specimen, a literary masterpiece, it is considered the pinnacle of the Victorian era—eccentric and dazzling, a kaleidoscope of imagery and plot.

You will find "The Return" eerie, a story with a majestic beginning—the setting a town that celebrates boundless joy and promises of success; the main characters helplessly in love yet adventurously searching for wealth—and a mystical ending surrounded by the mists and shadows of what could have been, sliced by what unfortunately is. The tension Gilchrist creates in this tiny story is formidable, and you will think about its outcome for days.

*F*ive minutes ago I drew the window curtain aside and let the mellow sunset light contend with the glare from the girandoles. Below lay the orchard of Vernon Garth, rich in heavily flowered fruit trees—yonder a medlar, here a pear, next a quince. As my eyes, unaccustomed to the day, blinked rapidly, the recollection came of a scene forty-five years past, and once more beneath the oldest tree stood the girl I loved, mischievously plucking yarrow, and, despite its evil omen, twining the snowy clusters in her black hair. Again her coquettish words rang in my ears: "Make me thy lady! Make me the richest woman in England, and I promise thee, Brian, we shall be the happiest of God's creatures." And I remembered how the mad thirst for gold filled me: how I trusted in her fidelity, and without reasoning or even telling her that I would conquer fortune for her sake, I kissed her sadly and passed into the world. Then followed a complete silence until the *Star of Europe*, the greatest diamond discovered in modern times, lay in my hand—a rough unpolished stone not unlike the lumps of spar I had often seen lying on the sandy lanes of my native county. This should be Rose's own, and all the others that clanked so melodiously in their leather bulse should go towards fulfilling her ambition. Rich and happy I should be soon, and should I not marry an untitled gentlewoman, sweet in her prime? The twenty years' interval of work and sleep was like a fading dream, for I was going home. The knowledge thrilled me so that my nerves were strung tight as iron ropes and I laughed like a young boy. And it was all because my home was to be in Rose Pascal's arms.

I crossed the sea and posted straight for Halkton village. The old hostelry was crowded. Jane Hopgarth, whom I remembered a ruddy-faced child, stood on the box-edged terrace, curtsying in matronly fashion to the departing mail-coach. A change in the signboard drew my eye; the white lilies had been painted over with a miter, and the name changed from the Pascal Arms to the Lord Bishop. Angrily aghast at this disloyalty, I cross-questioned the ostlers, who hurried to and fro, but failing to obtain any coherent reply I was fain to content myself with a mental denunciation of the times.

At last I saw Bow-Legged Jeffries, now bent double with age, sunning himself at his favorite place, the side of the horse trough. As of old he was chewing a straw. No sign of recognition came over his face as he gazed at me, and I was shocked, because I wished to impart some of my gladness to a fellow creature. I went to him, and after trying in vain to make him speak, held forth a gold coin. He rose instantly, grasped it with palsied fingers, and, muttering that the hounds were starting, hurried from my presence. Feeling half sad I crossed to the church-yard and gazed through the grated window of the Pascal burial chapel at the recumbent and undisturbed effigies of Geoffrey Pascal, gentleman, of Bretton Hall; and Margot Maltrevor his wife, with their quaint epitaph about a per-fect marriage enduring forever. Then, after noting the rank-ness of the docks and nettles, I crossed the worn stile and with footsteps surprisingly fleet passed towards the stretch of moorland at whose farther end stands Bretton Hall.

Twilight had fallen ere I reached the cottage at the entrance of the park. This was in a ruinous condition: here and there sheaves in the thatched roof had parted and formed crevices through which smoke filtered. Some of the tiny windows had been walled up, and even where the glass remained snakelike ivy hindered any light from falling into their thick recesses.

The door stood open, although the evening was chill. As I approached, the heavy autumnal dew shook down from the firs and fell upon my shoulders. A bat, swooping in an undulation, struck between my eyes and fell to the grass, moaning querulously. I entered. A withered woman sat beside the peat fire. She held a pair of steel knitting needles which she moved without cessation. There was no thread upon them, and when they clicked her lips twitched as if she had counted. Some time passed before I recognized Rose's foster mother, Elizabeth Carless. The russet color of her cheeks had faded and left a sickly grey; those sunken, dimmed eyes were utterly unlike the bright black orbs that had danced so mirthfully. Her stature, too, had shrunk. I was struck with wonder. Elizabeth could not be more than fifty-six years old. I had been away twenty years; Rose was fifteen when I left her, and I had heard Elizabeth say that she was only twenty-one at the time of her darling's weaning. But what a change! She had such an air of weary grief that my heart grew sick.

Advancing to her side I touched her arm. She turned, but neither spoke nor seemed aware of my presence. Soon, however, she rose, and helping herself along by grasping the scanty furniture, tottered to a window and peered out. Her right hand crept to her throat; she untied the string of her gown and took from her bosom a pomander set in a battered silver case. I cried out; Rose had loved that toy in her childhood; thousands of times we played ball with it. . . . Elizabeth held it to her mouth and mumbled it, as if it were a baby's hand. Maddened with impatience, I caught her shoulder and roughly bade her say where I should find Rose. But something awoke in her eyes, and she shrank away to the other side of the house-place: I followed; she cowered on the floor, looking at me with a strange horror. Her lips began to move, but they made no sound. Only when I crossed to the threshold did she rise; and then her head moved wildly from side to side, and her hands pressed close to her breast, as if the pain there were too great to endure.

I ran from the place, not daring to look back. In a few minutes I reached the balustraded wall of the Hell Garden. The vegetation there was wonderfully luxuriant. As of old, the great blue and white Canterbury bells grew thickly, and those curious flowers to which tradition has given the name of "Marie's Heart" still spread their creamy tendrils and blood-colored bloom on every hand. But "Pascal's Dribble," the tiny spring whose water pulsed so fiercely as it emerged from the earth, had long since burst its bounds, and converted the winter garden into a swamp, where a miniature forest of queen-of-the-meadow filled the air with melancholy sweetness. The house looked as if no careful hand had touched it for years. The elements had played havoc with its oriels, and many of the latticed frames hung on single hinges. The curtain of the blue parlor hung outside, draggled and faded, and half hidden by a thick growth of bindweed.

With an almost savage force I raised my arm high

above my head and brought my fist down upon the central panel of the door. There was no need for such violence, for the decayed fastenings made no resistance, and some of the rotten boards fell to the ground. As I entered the hall and saw the ancient furniture, once so fondly kept, now mildewed and crumbling to dust, quick sobs burst from my throat. Rose's spinet stood beside the door of the withdrawing room. How many carols had we sung to its music! As I passed my foot struck one of the legs and the rickety structure groaned as if it were coming to pieces. I thrust out my hand to steady it, but at my touch the velvet covering of the lid came off and the tiny gilt ornaments rattled downwards. The moon was just rising and only half her disc was visible over the distant edge of the Hell Garden. The light in the room was very uncertain, yet I could see the keys of the instrument were stained brown, and bound together with thick cobwebs.

Whilst I stood beside it I felt an overpowering desire to play a country ballad with an overword of "Willow browbound." The words in strict accordance with the melody are merry and sad by turns: at one time filled with light happiness, at another bitter as the voice of one bereaved forever of joy. So I cleared off the spiders and began to strike the keys with my forefinger. Many were dumb, and when I struck them gave forth no sound save a peculiar sigh; but still the melody rhythmed as distinctly as if a low voice crooned it out of the darkness. Wearied with the bitterness, I turned away.

By now the full moonlight pierced the window and quivered on the floor. As I gazed on the tremulous pattern it changed into quaint devices of hearts, daggers, rings, and a thousand tokens more. All suddenly another object glided amongst them so quickly that I wondered whether my eyes had been at fault—a tiny satin shoe, stained crimson across the lappets. A revulsion of feeling came to my soul and drove away all my fear. I had seen that selfsame shoe white and unsoiled twenty years before, when vain, vain Rose danced amongst her reapers at the harvest-home. And my voice cried out in ecstasy, "Rose, heart of mine! Delight of all the world's delights!"

She stood before me, wondering, amazed. Alas, so changed! The red-and-yellow silk shawl still covered her shoulders; her hair still hung in those eldritch curls. But the beautiful face had grown wan and tired, and across the forehead lines were drawn like silver threads. She threw her arms round my neck and, pressing her bosom heavily on mine, sobbed so piteously that I grew afraid for her, and drew back the long masses of hair which had fallen forward, and kissed again and again those lips that were too lovely for simile. Never came a word of chiding from them. "Love," she said, when she had regained her breath, "the past struggle was sharp and torturing—the future struggle will be crueler still. What a great love yours was, to wait and trust for so long! Would that mine had been as powerful! Poor, weak heart that could not endure!"

The tones of a wild fear throbbed through all her speech, strongly, yet with insufficient power to prevent her feeling the tenderness of those moments. Often, timorously raising her head from my shoulder, she looked about and then turned with a soft, inarticulate, and glad murmur to hide her face on my bosom. I spoke fervently; told of the years spent away from her; how, when working in the diamond fields she had ever been present in my fancy; how at night her name had fallen from my lips in my only prayer; how I had dreamed of her

amongst the greatest in the land—the richest, and, I dare
swear, the loveliest woman in the world. I grew warmer
still: all the gladness which had been constrained for so
long now burst wildly from my lips: a myriad of rich
ideas resolved into words, which, being spoken, wove
one long and delicious fit of passion. As we stood together, the moon brightened and filled the chamber with
a light like the day's. The ridges of the surrounding moorland stood out in sharp relief.

Rose drank in my declarations thirstily, but soon interrupted me with a heavy sigh. "Come away," she said
softly. "I no longer live in this house. You must stay with
me tonight. This place is so wretched now; for time, that
in you and me has only strengthened love, has wrought
much ruin here."

Half leaning on me, she led me from the precincts
of Bretton Hall. We walked in silence over the waste
that crowns the valley of the Whitelands and, being near
the verge of the rocks, saw the great pinewood sloping
downwards, lighted near us by the moon, but soon lost
in density. Along the mysterious line where the light
changed into gloom, intricate shadows of withered summer bracken struck and receded in a mimic battle. Before
us lay the Priests' Cliff. The moon was veiled by a grove
of elms, whose ever-swaying branches alternately increased and lessened her brightness. This was a place
of notoriety—a veritable Golgotha—a haunt fit only for
demons. Murder and theft had been punished here; and
to this day fireside stories are told of evil women dancing
round that Druids' circle, carrying hearts plucked from
gibbeted bodies.

"Rose," I whispered, "why have you brought me here?"

She made no reply, but pressed her head more closely

to my shoulder. Scarce had my lips closed ere a sound like the hiss of a half-strangled snake vibrated amongst the trees. It grew louder and louder. A monstrous shadow hovered above.

Rose from my bosom murmured, "Love is strong as Death! Love is strong as Death!"

I locked her in my arms, so tightly that she grew breathless. "Hold me," she panted. "You are strong."

A cold hand touched our foreheads so that, benumbed, we sank together to the ground, to fall instantly into a dreamless slumber.

When I awoke the clear grey light of the early morning had spread over the country. Beyond the Hell Garden the sun was just bursting through the clouds, and had already spread a long golden haze along the horizon. The babbling of the streamlet that runs down to Halkton was so distinct that it seemed almost at my side. How sweetly the wild thyme smelled! Filled with tender recollections of the night, without turning, I called Rose Pascal from her sleep.

"Sweetheart, sweetheart, waken! Waken! Waken! See how glad the world looks—see the omens of a happy future."

No answer came. I sat up, and looking round me saw that I was alone. A square stone lay near. When the sun was high I crept to read the inscription carved thereon:—
"Here, at four crosspaths, lieth, with a stake through the bosom, the body of Rose Pascal, who in her sixteenth year willfully cast away the life God gave."

About the Compiler

Kathleen Blease is a writer, editor, and collector of the classics. Her *love in Verse: Classic Poems of the Heart* is a *Boston Book Review* bestseller and called "poetic salve" by *Publishers Weekly*. Her other collections are *A Mother's Love: Classic Poems Celebrating the Maternal Heart* and *A Friend Is Forever: Precious Poems that Celebrate the Beauty of Friendship*. A stay-at-home mother and spare-time writer, Kathleen lives in the historic district of Easton, Pennsylvania, with her husband, Roger, and their two small sons, Ben and Max.